CHLOE'S FRIEND

Miss Chloe Branton has been found a position as a laundry maid in a wealthy country house. Although she dislikes the life, she respects her father's wishes, knowing the position will be temporary. Chloe has been placed there for her own safety — where the master of the house watches her. When she needs the help of the man she is falling in love with, Chloe does not know whether Mr Tobias Poole will betray her or be her friend . . .

VALERIE HOLMES

CHLOE'S FRIEND

Complete and Unabridged

LINFORD
Leicester

First published in Great Britain in 2010

First Linford Edition
published 2010

British Library CIP Data

Holmes, Valerie.
    Chloe's friend. - -
    (Linford romance library)
    1. Women household employees- -Fiction.
    2. Love stories. 3. Large type books.
    I. Title II. Series
    823.9'2–dc22

    ISBN 978–1–44480–413–3

Published by
F. A. Thorpe (Publishing)
Anstey, Leicestershire

Set by Words & Graphics Ltd.
Anstey, Leicestershire
Printed and bound in Great Britain by
T. J. International Ltd., Padstow, Cornwall

1

The laundry was unbearably hot. Chloe lifted the heavy sodden sheet from the line of scrub sinks into a tub used for doing hand washing, or in this instance, to lug the sheet to the big copper boiling pans above the oven. From here she would walk the four steps dragging her burden across the flagstone floor to Martha, the chief laundry maid, who was by the copper. Chloe had wanted to work in the kitchens. Instead, she worked by an oven fuelled by the wood from the estate with the two copper pans set into the wall above it. The larger pan boiled its load and the other was used for smaller washes.

The scrubbed sheet would soon be in the large copper pan. Chloe flopped them into the old tub and started to drag it across the floor. It was a hard task as there was a gradient and a channel allowing water to flow down to the drain under the sinks. Once it was in the pan it would boil for an hour whilst she turned her attention to rinsing the ones which had just finished their time. They still needed three rinses; she glanced at the mangle which she would have to use between each one, and sighed.

There was always food in a kitchen, she thought miserably to herself, and Chloe, despite her slight frame, always felt hungry.

'Jane, you have been told not to drag that; you must strengthen your body and carry it!' Martha snapped at her. 'Besides, girl, damage or split it and you'll be in hot water yourself.'

Chloe stood up to her full height of just under five feet tall and placed her hands on her narrow hips.

'I am Chloe, Martha. I am not called 'Jane', I am strong enough for a young woman and I have no intention of carrying anything so heavy when I can drag it there with half the effort.' Chloe flicked her loose dark brown hair out of her eyes with one quick movement of her head.

'Ee, lass, you have a mouth on you!' Martha stepped down from her perch where she had been reaching over the boiling water, tongs in hand, stirring in the lye which was needed to make the sheet white and clean again. Her arms were red and swollen, like her face, after years of doing the same thankless task. 'If Miss Ruddick hears you speak so wildly, you'll regret it. You've been given a place here at the hall, don't abuse it. You come from a shamed family, so lose your 'airs and graces' and work like the rest of us. You are too grand for your own good; that is why they've called you Jane — a simple name with no frills. Jane the laundrymaid, like Tilly and Mary, the lowest of the servants. So accept your lot and be grateful for it. Now, fetch that over here and carry it so that you become strong, for if you are to survive here, you best do as I say.' She placed her foot back on the small step ready to resume her position,

'I am Miss Chloe Branton. My family have done nothing wrong; my father just placed his faith in the wrong people and . . . '

Martha laughed at her and had to step down again. 'His faith left him long since. He paid men to steal goods and bring them in illegal like, whilst honest men fight Napoleon.'

'They were tradesmen, not thieves!' Chloe insisted, feeling her hot cheeks flush even more.

'Call a horse, a horse, and not a mule — stubborn as they are, just like you. He gave money to the Tillmans and everyone knew what their game was.' Martha stared her down.

'Well, Father didn't!' Chloe saw the open scorn on Martha's face.

'Well, shame on him then because he should have. Now, forget your past, lass. Your mother has picked up work making and mending in town. Your two brothers have gone to fight Napoleon in

Spain and you have been spared the workhouse by coming here whilst your father serves His Majesty in the navy. He was lucky not to be transported.' Martha shrugged. 'Better men have been sent to heathen places. No, he was lucky and that is the truth of it — as you have been also. I bet he moans about his lot, too. Nought as ungrateful as folk.'

'Father was a merchant seaman for years. He'll survive and he will come home safe. He never moaned.' Chloe's hands fell to her side. Listening to Martha speak of her lovely, happy family, spread as they were to the far corners of the earth, made her heart ache. She knew too well that her father was paying buying money, to the Tillmans, smugglers who had operated from the Bay towns on the north east coast. Her father had pulled 'strings' to find her this position and she should be grateful, but she wasn't. Chloe had wanted to look after her mother, be with her and care for her. She hated the hall, hated the feeling she should be at all thankful to them and hated the work. If that was not enough reason to be miserable she was forever hungry.

'Aye, well I hope he does. Now, 'Jane', Miss Ruddick will be here shortly and if you set lip to her like you just spoke to me then you'll feel the sharp edge of her tongue and will have no supper for a week.'

'Sorry, Martha, I don't mean to be rude to you, it is just that I miss my mother, Fred and Jimmy and I don't know if they are well.' Chloe stopped talking as her eyes were starting to feel watery. That was no good at all; it would serve no purpose other than to show how weak and vulnerable she felt. It was just not going to get her anywhere. She picked up the heavy tub and tried to adopt a strong countenance.

'That's a good lass. Look, wait till the old bag's been and I shall see if I can find you anything to nibble. But answer to Jane because if you don't you will lose your position here and end up on the streets.'

'Perhaps it would be better if I did!' Chloe slammed her load down on the stone floor.

'My girl, you can't be stupid enough as to believe that. However, that is your choice. If you'd prefer to lift your skirts for any jack-tar, who passes you a coin, then the choice is yours, but it isn't much of a life, believe me. I knew a girl who was caught thieving a piece of lace. Lied she did, said it had never been there, and then it was found under her mattress. Silly Peggy, she was turned out, with no reference or pay; she was sleeping anywhere she could with anyone who would pay her within weeks. Poor Peggy.' She shook her head.

'What happened to her?'

'Let's just say life on the streets is cold and short, too.' She raised an eyebrow at her as if understanding the futility of the reality of her situation.

'I'd never do that!' Chloe snapped indignantly.

'No, then how would you eat? Where would you live? Do you think young girls can just curl up anywhere and be safe? Lass, you'd be snapped up by folk you shouldn't know even exist. Your life started sweet. Now you have to work for a living, but don't throw it into the gutter or you'll live it there amongst the rats.'

Chloe helped the woman lift the sheet into the boiling water. She had a choice, she knew, stay or go. She'd never sell her favours, never, but Chloe had no idea if she dared make a break for freedom and take that first step into the unknown. A splash of the hot liquid caught her hand and she squealed.

'You'll have lots of them, girl.'

Chloe rubbed it and returned to the sinks when Miss Ruddick appeared at the door. Tall and austere, she brought in a young laundry maid who lived with her sister, Mary, in the nearby village. The girl was carrying a heavy load of even more soiled sheets and linen.

'Come on Jane, you can't dawdle

about all day. There's work to be done. Drop those down there, Tilly, Jane will see to them. Soak them in the cold tub for tomorrow and then you come with me. I have work Cook needs you to do.' She snapped her fingers and Tilly followed her out.

Chloe glared at her back. She had never hated anyone before in her life except the magistrate who had sent her father away, but next to him, her feelings for Miss Ruddick ran equally deep. Martha was absorbed with her copper, stirring with devotion. Chloe stared at the sheets still to soak, then the ones to rinse, and clenched her fists. She did have a choice to make whilst she still had a spirit in her left to save.

2

Tobias stooped low to check that the saddle was fastened securely and that the stable lad had been looking after his favourite mare correctly. He stroked the horse and was satisfied that the job had been done well when he heard the voice of Jimmy, the stable lad, as he entered the building. There was no reason why Tobias should hide; he was the overseer of the estate, but there was something about the way the lad was whispering which caught his attention.

'I tell thee, she is Branton's own daughter and he is working off his sins in HM's navy. He won't be back. They'll break him. Still, we have her here.'

'What if she is here? She is working now. There is no way she can contact her father or touch his stash, wherever he has it.' Will chuckled. 'Do you fancy her, Jimmy? Or are you after her father's money? If it existed her mother would not be sewing buttons on folks' clothes and mending things, would she?'

Tobias recognised the other voice as that of the young son of the local blacksmith. He'd obviously been sent from Gorebeck with the wagon to bring in his father's finished wares, as he also worked for the estate.

'Don't you realise what I mean? The Tillmans lost money, they had to change routes and move the goods that the revenue could not find. They've been put out and lost a boat and captain in the process, lots of things changed when they caught her father. Rumour even had it that the man done a deal to save his skin and that of his wife and girl. If they can lay their hands on that young miss she'll go missing for sure. They are angry, desperate men. They lost face with their suppliers across the German Sea and to make up they'd sell anything.'

Tobias slowly stood up having heard quite enough of the lad's wild ramblings, but he still could not be seen over the side of the stall.

'You don't know nothing. You are always spinning a yarn, Jimmy. Gossip is all you hears and titbits of stories from those tales that the young misses read. Nah, don't look surprised. People talk and the master found that young Miss Clarrissa drooling over some tale of a fair maiden being kidnapped by a dark wastrel. She was taken to the vicarage and made to repent. So stop spreading more trouble.' He laughed, 'Perhaps you could tell this to the young Miss because, after all, she has been banned from reading the novellas so you could share your lurid tales instead.' He chuckled.

The tone of Jimmy's voice changed. It was more authoritative, deeper and held a serious note. The smile on Tobias' face also vanished.

'I know the facts. You listen to tittle-tattle if you must, but I know that girl will be in grave danger if they find where she's been hidden, so keep that mouth or yours shut, Will. Don't even tell your pa.'

'They can't sell a white woman. Are you mad?' Young Will's voice rose an octave as he whispered, trying to hide the excitement that the conversation was having upon two young impressionable males.

'You're wrong! I knew of a woman who had been brought back on a ship. She was returned to her, family, but spent her days muttering about corsairs. No one understood her thinking she had lost someone in France. They thought she was mad. Turned out she had been all the way to Turkey, kidnapped from a port by Barbary corsairs, taken past France, and had only been rescued when an Englishman saw her in a market and smuggled her back on his ship. I tell you, the Tillmans know folk in Hull who'll do this if the price is good enough,' Jimmy said with total conviction.

'How do you know all this, Jimmy?' Will asked, which was just before Tobias had the chance to interrupt, giving his presence away. He had never been an eavesdropper or peeping Tom but what had appeared to start out as a momentary interest — a joke between two young friends — had turned into something much more serious. What he wasn't sure was quite what, as they were just lads, how much should he believe? The boy knew far more than he should about a trade which had been largely ignored, but had existed for centuries.

'I know because my mother is now married to Joe Tillman, Henry's son. He works over at Whitby in the shipyards, building and repairing cobles. I see her every three months and she tells me what's been happening. He works there as it gives him even more contacts and is useful to the family. But you keep your mouth tight shut or I'll send 'em to you, you hear?'

'Blood honour, Jimmy,' the lad said

solemnly. 'Blood honour!'

'Aye, blood honour, Will. Don't mention about the Branton girl, not to no one. Don't want her on our conscience, do we? Besides,' Jimmy laughed, 'she's quite skinny, so, no, I don't fancy her. Too full of herself by all accounts.'

The two walked out of the stable and Tobias heard the wagon move off. After a few moments whilst he gathered his thoughts he led the horse out. Jimmy had gone with his friend in the wagon and would no doubt run back to the stables from the end of the drive. Tobias mounted the horse, his mind mulling over what he had just heard. Did the lad speak the truth? If so, he needed to take action, but what specifically and how? He looked at the great hall, built from the proceeds of commerce. That same commercial success gleaned from cotton, sugar and slaves. Would the master really care if a few unlucky wenches were traded overseas instead of finding themselves steeped in gin in the brothels here? How could he approach anyone and say he believed that someone may be in peril on the basis of the conversation between two lads. He clenched a fist around the reins. He had seen enough violence and abuse when he served in the cavalry for Sir Arthur Wellesley. This position was supposed to be a step away from all the bloodshed he had seen in India and France.

Tobias rode off down the drive. He had work to do and real issues to deal with, not pondering the ramblings of a boy's imagination.

The image of the slaves he had seen in the port of Bristol came to his mind. It abhorred him; he knew there was a trade in women. It was not on the same scale and was not spoken about in the same way, but he had seen evidence of it. He would introduce himself to the girl when he returned and make sure she was safe, just in case.

He shook his head and kicked the horse on. He'd see the tenants first about the broken plough and then he'd go by the laundry later and see if she was there.

The thought of returning to the hall via the laundry did not please him, He usually avoided any contact with Miss Ruddick. She grimaced at him; it was the nearest she could get to a smile but it made his flesh creep because he knew she would like to befriend him. He needed no friends like her. He did not want to join forces — overseer and head of the maids! To her it might be an ideal match; to him it would be suffocating. He liked to be free. No woman would pin him down. He had loved and lost once — that would not happen to Tobias Poole again.

He passed Jimmy as he was walking back to the hall. He touched his cap at Tobias without a care in the world.

'Jimmy, come to the stables after you've eaten.'

'Am I in trouble, Mr Poole?' The lad looked worried.

'I don't know, are you?' Tobias asked.

'No, sir,' he said quickly, almost too quickly,

'Then why ask?'

The lad shrugged and nodded. Tobias rode beyond the gates, galloping with the wind in his face wondering why he was getting himself involved with something that could only spell trouble for him. A woman was trouble and the daughter of a financier of a contraband ring was definitely going to pose a challenge.

He let the horse have its head and grinned; he had forgotten just how much he enjoyed a challenge.

3

Chloe struggled to carry the large basket full of dirty linen that she was to remove from the kitchens. It was her duty to return with it to the laundry once the clean had been replaced in the cupboard. From here the upstairs servants would move it to wherever it needed to be in the house.

She had lingered longer than she should have as she delivered the freshly ironed linen and carefully placed each piece in the cupboard in the corridor outside the dairy room. The cupboard had been installed here so that it was near the stairs which led up to the hall and the central stairs. She had never been allowed up there. It was not her place. Mary and Tilly had returned to the village, which left her to finish tidying up. Chloe thought differently to them. They accepted their lot having

19

known no other. She had once slept in a bed covered with linen and lace. Sarah, her maid, had warmed it for her with a bedpan. Her life had not been in a grand hall but a large town house. She looked at her aching fingers as she touched the delicate lace and all manner of starched pieces that were now left neatly on the shelves.

Memories flooded back to her of her family and then another pain replaced her nostalgia — hunger. Chloe loved the smells which emanated from the large kitchen where Cook worked away constantly preparing, baking or cooking food for the family. Her team were efficient and hard working, but also well fed. She made sure that her staff had decent food and was quoted as saying that they cannot work on empty bellies — not when their work is with food. Cook's stomach certainly was not empty.

'Branton!' Cook's voice bellowed out from the dairy.

Chloe shut the cupboard door and

ran to the open stone archway of the dairy. 'Yes, Mrs Hebden, do you need me?' she spoke quietly.

'Did you fall asleep, lass? I could have washed, dried, starched and ironed the whole cupboard's worth of linen in the time you have played around with it. If Miss Ruddick finds you lazing around you will be up all night doing the worst of soiled dirties she can find.'

Chloe looked down, she hated being rebuked and had to avert her eyes or risk another sterner ticking off for arrogance, as her eyes often betrayed her defiance. Humility was something that came hard to her as a servant. The kitchen servants were above her in status, the upper house servants were above them, and so she must be humble and lowly.

'Look at you, girl! I have seen brooms with more width. Here, but eat it quickly and don't let Ruddick find you or I will say you took it without my knowledge. I shall not stand in trouble for a chit like you. Do something with that hair of yours, it is as wilful as its owner.' She shoved a small bowl into Chloe's hand which had a large dollop of thick, rich, buttery cream in it. Before Chloe could say, 'thank you', she was left alone.

Chloe knew too well the rivalry between the two women. Cook was the lowest of the upper house servants and Ruddick was the chambermaid, responsible for the lower servants. She had snapped Chloe up from Cook's grasp as her request for an extra pair of hands had been heard first. That had grated on Cook. Mindful of the warning she had just received, she ate up the cream, savouring every last lick using her finger to clean out the bowl. It was smooth, lovely and gone all too soon. She left the bowl on the side and ran out across the cobbled yard, as fast as she could, carrying the basket of laundry. If she cut across by the stable, through the bell tower arch, she would be back in the laundry room before Miss Ruddick came to see if it had all been swabbed out. Then, after her supper, thankfully, she could climb the wooden steps to the warm room she shared with Martha above the laundry itself. Martha liked to be warm so she always let the fire burn as long as she could. That way the heat of the water would still keep their room cosy as long as possible. Chloe was lost in thought, wondering if she would ever have a decent sleep in her life again, as Martha snored like a trooper. She wasn't sure how troopers snored but it was what her mother had always said.

She lugged the basket but her hair flicked across her eyes, escaping from the cap. She tried to hurry and slipped, letting out a yelp like a puppy, just as a horse and rider appeared through the arch of the bell tower.

'Are you all right, miss?' Tobias asked.

'You scared me!' She glared up at him then stared at the laundry basket which was now laid on its side with the contents spilled over the cobblestones.

She pulled off her cap, which had slipped also when she misplaced her footing and, with hands on hips, hair falling over her shoulder, she sighed. 'Now, I'm really for it!'

'Jane! Jane! You disgraceful girl! When will you learn to behave any better than a common street woman? Place that cap back on your head immediately! Are you shameless?' Miss Ruddick's voice barked from the shadows of the bell tower. Like an apparition, materialising from a murky past she appeared.

'I . . . he . . . ' She looked momentarily into the rider's eyes, noting a spark of amusement. Ruddick was striding over. Much as it hurt her pride to do so, she dropped her hands to her side, averted her eyes and quietly muttered, 'Sorry, Miss Ruddick'.

'It is I who should apologise, ma'am. I fear I rode in rather carelessly and scared her.'

Chloe was surprised he had spoken up,

'No . . . No . . . Mr Poole, for Jane should have been long finished and she has no business carrying her work across the open yard. Servants are not supposed to make a spectacle of themselves in public. Thank goodness the family are at dinner.'

The mention of food made Chloe almost swoon. The cream was so lovely yet not enough to sustain her.

'Tonight, my girl, you shall scrub these before you go to bed and leave them to soak overnight. Forget supper for you. An empty stomach might just remind you to take care in future.'

Chloe's mouth dropped open as she stared at the woman who daily she learned to hate more.

'Cover that hair! You look like a Jezebel.'

Chloe's chin rose slightly upwards, deep blue eyes rising to a challenge. She would not be spoken to in such a fashion, but before she revealed what was on her mind, Mr Poole shook his head at her. He was behind Miss

Ruddick, who could not see his warning being given.

Chloe flipped her hair back, swept it together at the nape of her neck and replaced her bonnet as quickly as she could. Now the man who had watched her every gesture was openly smiling at her. However, Ruddick's face was set like the stone of the hall.

'Get these items up and laundered tonight, I do not want to see or hear you again today. You have vexed me, child.' She turned to look up at Mr Poole.

Chloe bent down and did as she had been ordered whilst he dismounted and, accompanied by Miss Ruddick, walked his horse over to the stable block. Chloe's cheeks burned. Don't they make a fine pair, she thought sarcastically to herself. He, a fine looking man in his prime. She knew her thoughts were tainted with a hint of jealousy, singularly unattractive in a female, her father would have said. Poole was strong as he held on to his mount, yet she had noticed how agile he was as he dismounted. Ruddick was quite different, where Tobias was dark in colouring with deep brown hair, she had mousy coloured straight thick hair pulled back into an inescapable bun beneath her uniform cap. Also tall, slim, straight of back, Chloe had to admit she held herself well, but then she did not have to stoop to carry such burdens as her and the other under servants, the dairy maids. Chloe, too, felt Miss Ruddick belonged above stairs and not as a servant. It made her wonder what her story was. In Chloe's eyes everyone had one. Hers had turned sour as fate had decided to smite her family, but what was Ruddick's? She must remember to ask Martha.

Two long hours later the house was quiet. Servants had finally finished their chores and were returning to slumber for a few hours before they were up again at four or five in the morning, ready to restart the same cycle. The laundry would have been silent also, except for Chloe's sighs, sobs and grunts, and Martha's snoring from behind the wooden door. In the candle light it was difficult to see what she had made clean and what was still stained.

'Still scrubbing? You'll ruin your hands.'

Mr Poole's voice made her jump and drop the block of lye soap she was using. He bent down and picked it up. 'Here,' he said softly as he placed it in her hand. His eyes looked directly into hers; she saw the humour in them disperse. How could he not notice that she had been crying? His touch lingered as he inspected her hand.

Chloe took the soap from him and pulled her fingers from his.

'Your hands are not used to this kind of work, are they?' He leaned against the doorway and folded his arms.

She threw the soap back into the water in a futile pique of temper. Only half her chore had been completed. She ached, her stomach felt empty and her spirits were as low and dark as the cloud covered sky.

'I'm busy.' She had not meant to snap the words out but if he was trying to dally with her he could find some other amusement she was not in the mood to be teased, it was all she could do to prop herself up against the row of scrub sinks.

He walked inside and picked up Miss Ruddick's chair from over near the airers and placed it behind Chloe. 'Sit before you fall down, Chloe.'

'I've work to finish,' she complained. 'You called me Chloe.'

'It is your name, is it not?' he asked.

'Everyone has been told to call me 'Jane' because they think I am to be plain and simple.'

'Sit,' he said firmly, but kept his voice low as he placed a hand on her shoulder and pulled her back. He then stepped in front of her and rolled up his shirt sleeves. 'I should think you are neither plain nor simple, Chloe Branton. However, you are out of your depth at the moment and sinking, slowly but surely.'

'What are you doing, sir?' she asked. Even though her head ached she tried to stand up. With one finger pressing on her shoulder he sent her body back down to the chair.

'I need to wash my hands,' he grinned. For a moment he stepped back outside and brought in a small bread basket, closing the door behind him. He also brought in a lantern which he lit once inside. 'I had a word with Mrs Hebden; she has a good heart and a large pantry. Here are some titbits for you: cold mutton, cheese, soft bread and a small jug of her husband Tommy's ale. You feast yourself and I'll have these sorted in no time.' He turned to the sink and, with one flourish, poured the rest of the washing into it.

'You like doing laundry — a woman's work? Do you know how? If you ruin anything I shall be blamed. Why would you?'

'Eat, before your voice wakes up

Martha.' He started to scrub and with deft hands showed he knew very well how to wash, scrub and was strong enough to make each sodden bundle look as though it floated on air when he lifted it. 'In the army you learn many things.'

'Why would you do this for me? I thought you and the banshee were friends . . . ' She paused, as she realised the ale had freed her tongue and the food had quenched her hunger.

He turned around, flicked water at her and ignored the comments. It was difficult for Chloe to say what happened next because she had no memory of it. Exhaustion and ale make strange bedfellows. However, when she awoke the next morning atop her cot she heard Martha shouting her from down in the laundry. She should have been awake earlier, much earlier. It was her job to fill the copper with cold water and start the fire going so that when Martha arose an hour later the water would be already hot.

Chloe had almost decided that she had had the strangest of dreams, but was greeted by the sight of Martha staring around her as the linen above was hung on racks suspended over her head. The floor, which had been swabbed down was dry like the sinks and even the tongs were uniformly arranged alongside each other.

'Ee, lass, you are full of surprises. Go brush your hair and look under my pillow. I saved you a piece of parkin from last night. Eat it quickly and be down here like will-o-the-wisp.' She sent her off quickly.

Chloe turned and realised that the steam was rising from the copper. He had even set it going, the man must have had little sleep. She washed her face, and smelt her hands. Something felt different about them. The cracks were not so dry, The skin felt as if balm had been applied. Had Tobias Poole done that? Why? She brushed her hair and pinned it into her bonnet then guiltily ate every last crumb of the parkin, as obviously Martha had no knowledge of her visitor or of the feast he had brought her. Chloe smiled as he made her way back down the stairs, but then was struck by a thought which made her scared. This stranger had done her a great favour; nobody did work for free . . . so what would he want from her in return?

4

Two days later she finally saw Mr Poole riding over the fields beyond the walled garden. She had been sent to find the lavender which the gardener had promised them earlier in the week and had forgotten to deliver. She almost ran along by the east wall and then waited to catch her breath before walking beyond the corner and into his sights as he rode towards her.

He stopped his horse as she knew instinctively he would. During the previous day at some time, someone had put a little pot of home-made balm, which smelt of thyme and other herbs, in her laundry basket.

'Good day . . . Jane.'

'Thank you, Mr Poole,' she said bluntly, staring up at him, and was surprised when he slid down off the horse and stood not two feet from her.

'You know I can never repay your kindness . . . in any way.'

He smiled at her. 'I have not asked you to, have I? Are you always so defensive, Jane?'

'No, not yet. My name is Chloe, as you know.'

'Keep the name whilst you are here, it may not suit you, but it is a good idea to be, in a way, anonymous.'

'Yes, as I have no choice. I am a woman on her own, so I am defensive. What else can I do?' She did not wait for him to answer. 'Thank you, for your kindness.' She stared at him, but as he studied her, she felt awkward and tried to walk on.

'You were at breaking point.' He stroked his horse's neck. 'Horses need to be broken to be beasts of burden, not young women. I caused you to spill your load, and so, I made things right.' He winked at her. 'As right as they can be.'

'The balm, you left it, didn't you?' She felt bolder now.

'Yes, you need to protect your delicate skin against the constant water and heat.' He looked away at some ducks flying past.

'Do you envy them, Chloe Branton? Do you wish you could be free like them?' He watched her face as if studying her expression.

'Yes,' she said with conviction.

'Then next time you feel tempted to fly off, remember that the hunter often shoots them down. Think twice, Chloe Branton, and be content to be Jane for now. See what tomorrow brings, and look after those hands of yours. They may one day return to grander things.'

She laughed at him and he took a step back as if abashed by her levity, then remounted.

'You dream more than I do, do you not, Mr Poole?' She smiled at him as he peered down at her.

'Take care, some dreams become nightmares. If you need me, my room is above the bell tower arch, use the steps nearest the stables.'

'Are you expecting me to come to your private quarters?' she asked, wondering if he was expecting her to give him favour.

'You must learn to listen, Jane. I said if you need me, not if I want you.' He touched the broad rim of his hat and rode off, leaving Chloe most puzzled by his comments, even more so than his actions.

5

The night Chloe discovered she had a friend in the mysterious Mr Poole, Jimmy had entered the stables nervously as he been ordered to do after seeing Will off earlier in the day. However, he was to be surprised when Poole did not appear. Jimmy had then gone to Poole's room over the archway of the bell tower, the bell having long since been silenced as it had annoyed the family. Jimmy could not find him there either as his door was shut and there was no answer from inside. He knew better than to try and open it. Even if there was no lock, there were boundaries and the door was one definite one not to be crossed unless invited inside.

Jimmy had decided that the elusive Mr Poole must have been summoned by someone himself. The lad had run back down the stairs, the house was quiet at that late hour and he was tired; the only light he saw was a glimmer from behind the old shutters in the laundry. Strange, he had thought, because they should also be long abed. Giving in to a natural curiosity he put his fatigue aside and instead crept around the outside of the inner yard, past the potting shed and along the wall of the laundry buildings, stopping only to peer through a crack within the shutter. He had found Tobias Poole, and what else had he discovered? The man was carrying the Branton wench up the steps. She seemed to lay relaxed in his arms, not moving or struggling away from his body. He saw Ruddick's chair gently rocking and guessed they had found it very cosy. A soldier knows his way with women and this one had looks and a style of his own. He knew he'd been in the cavalry as he had come across his sword, by chance of course, but the man said little of his past. Just rode around like he owned the place. He watched them and then leaned back. No struggle there then, Jimmy had thought, and laughed silently to himself, as even from outside he heard Martha's snores from her bed. The old hag had no idea what went on in her own rooms.

Jimmy ran silently back to his own cot in the stables. If he told the master about them they could both lose their positions. Knowledge, as he had often been told by his betters, was a valuable thing, but not for the likes of him. Jimmy was a lad who knew lots of things; he collected information like scraps tossed from his master's table. He would wait till his newly acquired knowledge was worth something to him, and then he would share it. Until then he would keep it to himself, satisfied that now he had something he could use over Poole, and how he would.

★　★　★

Tobias stared out of his window. He had been kept up late as there had been a problem with one of the tenants which had required his attendance. Jake had drunk the rent money, leaving his family on the verge of being thrown out of their one room cottage. Tobias could either evict the family, as his master would have had him do, or have the blighter thrown in the village lock up to sober up. He was going to let him out at mid-day and then make him work like he was in the army. The man was not going to know what had hit him, other than the back of Tobias' hand if he had anymore problems from him. Jake had a wife and two children to feed. He was lucky to have a tenancy and land to till. This was his last chance. Tobias did not want to throw the woman and children into the workhouse but Jake was a drunkard, he either shaped up or walked.

Tobias found himself watching the Branton girl as she scurried along by the potting shed making her way to the back of the hall. She was more than a girl, he knew that, but by thinking of her in those terms he felt protective towards her instead of feeling attracted. He didn't want to become fond of any woman. This one was small of frame, shapely he had discovered as he carried her, but had an inner strength. She had hair that when loose hung wild, eyes that stared into a man's heart and a iron-clad determination. He wondered how long it would be before that strength of character led her to do something rash. He was sure she had no intention of staying, but Jimmy's words about the Tillmans haunted him. The boy was not just spreading lies and fancy tales. Tobias knew enough to recognise the truth in his words and he was only too aware of the Tillmans' reputation. He was about to turn away from his window when he saw Jimmy leaning against the end of the potting shed. The lad waited until Chloe stepped past it and then surprised her as he spoke to her. Whatever it was caused her to spin around quickly, words were exchanged which resulted in her storming off. The boy appeared to find their exchange funny and sauntered slowly towards the stables.

Tobias put his hat on his head, slipped his riding jacket on and made his way down. If that little runt thought he was going to toy with her because he knew who her father was, he was in for a surprise. She was already trapped. Tobias didn't want her to spring it prematurely and disappear into the night, never to be seen again. He ran down the stairs and strode over to the stables just as Jimmy walked in.

★ ★ ★

Chloe had not understood what the lad was getting at, but she hadn't liked his manner. Why should she be looking for 'Tobias'. It had taken her a minute to realise that he had been referring to Mr Poole. He had been smug, almost laughing in her face. Had he known that she had been helped by him? Why the familiarity either in the boy's manner when speaking to her or by using Mr Poole's Christian name? No, he was angling for something. She knew what she would like to give him beyond the piece of advice she did about using proper titles when addressing his betters, but that like everything else she wanted to do, she could not.

She stopped before going to the lower servants' door below the ground level of the hall. The proper entrances were for the family only. The servants were to be as invisible and silent as possible.

The grounds were vast. She knew people were starving elsewhere in city hovels, yet here the grounds were cared for with love and an army of servants just to please one family. It was all wrong but it was the way of the world. Chloe realised she was being watched.

She turned, expecting to see Miss Ruddick there ready to give her another telling off for dawdling and then set her a task that would take her into the small hours before storming off in high dudgeon, but instead she found herself facing a young gentleman dressed for riding in the finest attire, carrying a silver topped riding crop in his hand.

He was staring at her. She immediately dipped the tiniest of curtsies and took brisk steps towards the servants' lower stairs.

'Wait!' he snapped. She realised he must be the master's son, and stopped instantly.

'I'm sorry, sir. I am new here. I missed the stairs.' She pointed behind her. 'It will never happen again.'

He smiled at her, obviously amused. Here she was, scared, powerless against his actions as he was a man with a position in society and he found her amusing. He reminded her of a cat as it toyed with a mouse, knowing it held its fate in its whim.

'You are new here, aren't you?' His head was held naturally high that it was as if he was speaking to someone behind her.

'Yes, sir.' She stepped back.

'Are you one of the creatures from the laundry?'

Chloe could hardly believe her ears because he had not even realised the insult he gave. To him she was a 'creature'.

'No, sir. That is, I work in the laundry, but I don't believe myself to be a 'creature'.' She wished she had controlled her tongue but there it was said.

'Well, I never, a spirited maid. I shall sleep soundly tonight, knowing that such a creature has held my sheets in her hands. We are all God's creatures child — only some more so than others! Get about your business, wench, and never let yourself be found here again, and curb that tongue or I shall have to take you to task.' He turned around and

46

walked to the mounting block waiting, swishing his crop as he went.

Chloe ran down the stairs, her heart pounding, her choices becoming more urgent as each day passed by.

6

Jimmy entered the stable with a very confident air about him. His smile appeared broader than usual, he twirled a blade of grass carelessly between his fingers as he approached Tobias and then looked him straight in the eye. 'Did you want something?' he asked casually.

Tobias was no man's fool, certainly no boy's one, he knew when trouble was near. ''Sir', you forgot the word, 'sir'.'

'Did I?' Jimmy calmly swaggered past Tobias and went over to his cot which was placed against the side of the far stall of the stables. Here he sat himself down. 'No, I don't think I did.' He had been allowed to use this unneeded space as his until, or if, it was ever wanted for another mount. This was unlikely because the house had more horses than it had family members, and there was little need of them all, particularly as Miss Clarissa did not like riding, so her horse had an easy life.

Tobias followed him and stood square in the opening, blocking the entrance or, as Tobias planned, Jimmy's possible hasty retreat. Whatever this cocky upstart thought he was doing, he was about to get a huge wake-up call. 'Whilst your head still rests upon your shoulders, Jimmy, apologise to me and give me the courtesy of the respect my position demands, or explain yourself fully. But be quick about it because you have one minute in which to do so before that head is knocked from its perch.' Tobias noticed a moment of doubt cross the lad's face.

'I will call you 'sir' when we can be heard by others, but between us, Tobias, things are going to change,' Jimmy crossed his arms in front of his body and stood as tall as he could.

'Explain your words, James, with

great care and haste . . . think before you speak again,' Tobias said, and moved further into the entrance of the stall.

'You see, you need me to be a good friend to you. Friends trust one another. They look out for each other and share their booty. They cover for each other.'

'Why would I need a friend like you?' His voice was calm. He felt as though he was being primed for blackmail, yet could not begin to imagine what the lad thought he had on him. Yes, he had a past, but it was buried deep, beyond the reach of this scrap of manhood and even the Tillmans.

'You like your position here, don't you?'

Tobias wanted to whack Jimmy, and wipe that cockiness from his lips, but he was intrigued by the sheer audacity and stupidity of him. He needed to be taught a lesson, one he would not forget and one which would, if he took heed, prevent him from taking another fall for years to come. 'Yes.'

'Well, Tobias, you be good to me, as a friend should be and share, and I shall keep my mouth firmly shut about you and the Branton wench.' He leaned forward and added, 'Don't want to get Miss Ruddock jealous, do we?'

'You make no sense, boy. Have you been at Tommy's ale, or perhaps you just plain lost your senses?' Tobias saw that his own composure was starting to have an unnerving effect upon Jimmy.

'I saw you the other night in the laundry. I saw you carry her up the steps. I know what you'd been doing, but I won't say a word so long as you are good to me, eh?' He smiled, but there was a nervous twitch to his lip.

Tobias didn't smile back. 'You think you have the measure of me, do you? You have just made one mistake, boy, a very big mistake.' He grabbed Jimmy's ear and dragged him out of the stall, the lad started whimpering and cursing in turn. Tobias then frog-marched him by the scruff of his collar over to Miss

Ruddick's small room, pushing the door open and forcing a very confused Jimmy inside.

'Mr Poole, whatever is the matter?' She was on her feet in an instant.

'I apologise for my interruption, Miss Ruddick but we have an issue to clear up which would tarnish my reputation and that of one of your laundry maids.' Miss Ruddick put down her book by her lamp and stared at a wide-eyed Jimmy.

'I know what I saw!' he yelped.

Tobias almost threw him to the floor. 'Miss Ruddick, this peeping Tom was snooping around the laundry three nights since. If you remember you had set the girl, Jane, extra work for being clumsy in the yard. I saw from my window that the candles were still flickering in there in the early hours of the morning. I went over and surely enough she had done her task but had fallen asleep in the chair. I couldn't rouse her so carried her up the steps, and awoke Martha who saw to the lass, whilst I extinguished the candles below before leaving. This sorry excuse for a servant saw her being carried up the steps and has accused me and the lass, who knew nothing of it, of impropriety. I ask you, Miss Ruddick, to take care and guard against any such gossip, but I have now a dilemma. Do I tell the master that he has a sneak working in his stable yard or do we think of a suitable punishment and teach the lad a lesson?' Tobias and Miss Ruddick looked down upon a very anxious Jimmy.

'But I thought . . . you had her in your arms . . . and . . . '

'How else do you carry someone?' Tobias remarked, a rhetorical question. He looked at Miss Ruddick with innocence and disbelief and then glanced skywards.

The woman was in her element. He had come to her and explained himself, asking for her opinion and support. 'We should not bother the master. It would be an unnecessary stress for him. No,

Jimmy, you can apologise now to Mr Poole and then once your work is done at the stables, you can come to me. Tommy was telling me that the potting shed was in a mess. It is time it was completely swept out and sorted. Each night this week you will help to sort, scrub and clean it. You will order all the pots by size and type. Once he is satisfied the job is complete you will then return to your normal duties and you will never set foot near my laundry or my girls again.' She leaned over to him. 'And if you ever spread lies and gossip I personally will take the block of lye and wash out that filthy mouth of yours. Now stand up and stop snivelling!'

Jimmy stood up. 'Sorry . . . sir,' he muttered, 'Ma'am.'

Tobias nodded. 'Go back to the stables. I want it completely mucked out, scrubbed and fresh hay in there tomorrow. You best sleep sound because tomorrow you are going to be very busy. Idle hands make for idle gossip.

Go!' Jimmy almost ran from the room, face flushed and defeated.

'Thank you, Miss Ruddick, and I do apologise for disturbing you.'

'It is no bother, Mr Poole, but if I may make so bold as to reprimand you in the mildest form. Please, if such an unusual occurrence should ever happen again, come for me and I will deal with it. I would hate your good name to be marred by gossip — especially if it were to be linked to a lowly laundry maid.' She stood before him. 'Sir, it would be her ruin and your reputation would suffer, your position could be lost to you.'

He smiled at her, aware that she was so close, and realising he had played his bluff as far as he dare. 'I thank you for your understanding, and I fear I must leave now because I would hate to tarnish your good reputation by lingering here a while more than provident.' He bowed slightly and left.

Tobias made straight for the laundry. 'Martha, could I have a word, please?'

She stepped into the drying room and he explained what he had just told Miss Ruddick.

'I knew that lass could no more clear that load on her own. You did it. It was you . . . soft in the head you must be. I bet you didn't own up to that.' She shook her head. 'Lordy, you are supposed to be a tough, hard man.'

'I am when I need to be, but it was my fault that she dropped her basket in the first place so the punishment was rightly mine, and besides she was halfway through. Here, Martha, take this, I handed her to you and you laid her on her cot. She was exhausted and knew nothing of it.' He gave Martha a coin which would ensure she corroborated his story, as he knew Miss Ruddick would check it out.

'Right, but you stay out of my room and keep your hands off the lass; she would not survive the streets if she loses her job here. Remember Betty? Who was it that gave her a babe, eh? You tell me that because she dared not.'

'It was NOT me!' he said. 'Nothing untoward happened between me and Chloe, I never knew Betty. I only laid her down on her cot because she was exhausted. Now, I must go before Ruddick sees me in here. She is far from slow. Watch out for Jimmy, Martha, he tried to blackmail me and he has connections with the Tillmans. If you hear anything concerning him tell me straight away.'

Martha nodded and then made sure the way was clear for Tobias to slip out.

Chloe came down the steps from their room and before her foot touched the floor Martha was there. 'Girl, I want words with you, private like!'

7

Chloe had heeded Martha's warning. She had been careless when Mr Poole had appeared and offered to help. However, the food he had brought and the help he had given had been gratefully received and much needed. Martha was worried that Chloe had let her guard down and allowed a man to come close to her. The memory of the fate of the woman, Betty, obviously still haunted Martha so Chloe accepted her advice and reproof in good faith. She was more concerned about being seen by the young master of the house than being carried by Tobias Poole. Why, she did not know on either account, but she was a creature of instinct — that word 'creature' was it really how he looked upon his servants, or was it a fashionable turn of phrase? Chloe, suitably chastised, returned to her tasks.

★　★　★

Tobias Poole returned to the stables where Jimmy had begun the first of his monumental jobs.

The lad looked up at him as he entered. Tobias saw the emotion in his eyes, hatred burned within him. 'Do you still want to call me 'Tobias'?' he asked.

Jimmy shook his head.

'Pardon?' Tobias stressed the point, he would be spoken to with respect.

'No, sir. That is not what I want to call you.' He continued raking out the hay.

'Good.' Tobias stifled a smile at the unspoken words in the lad's heart. He would like to call him a lot more.

'But, sir, I know what I saw and there was plenty of work left to be done when I left. The 'truth' has been washed away with the wench's washing.'

Jimmy's feet were lifted from the ground as Tobias grabbed him by his waistcoat and slammed him against the

59

stable wall. 'Listen, lad, I have fought wars against real men, you would be a fool to make threats against me. You keep that nose of yours out of other people's affairs and tame that tongue. Cross me again and you'll be glad to be able to muck out stables. You think you know people and things. I know far worse. I have lived through hell, so don't think you can better me with blackmail. Now finish your jobs with some humility and don't speak to me like that again. You have been let off lightly this time. You did see the woman in my arms, Jane is a lady, not a common whore, treat her with respect and keep her name safe. If she goes missing you will be my first port of call.'

Jimmy's eyes widened as those words were said. Tobias released him. He was averse to using his strength against anyone if it was not a fair match, but he had to make the lad see sense.

'What do you mean — go missing?' Jimmy asked.

'Exactly that.' He watched Jimmy

fumble with the end of the broom.

'I wouldn't have spragged on either of you. I just wanted more victuals and an easier life, that's all. I'd not tell on her. She could be in danger, I know that. Her father upset the Tillmans and she is here. I think she is in hiding, whether she knows it or not.'

'Then let us give her the benefit of the doubt. We can be like guardian angels keeping a discreet watch over her. I have connections also, Jimmy, but I don't want to use them if not needed, but you learn a lesson from today. Don't step beyond your means. I could eat you up and spit you out and yet in your over-rated confidence you tried to control me. Learn some wisdom. You are lucky you haven't had the thrashing of your life.' Tobias could see genuine regret in Jimmy's face. 'So will you tell your step-father about her?'

Jimmy's mouth dropped open. 'You know who he is!'

'Aye, lad, I know.'

Jimmy shook his head. 'Never. Why

do you think I work here? I hate him, but he is good to Ma.'

'Then stop confiding in others. That way you know how far your secret is hidden. Do you think the master would want you here if he knew who your family was?' Tobias saw a crestfallen expression replace all other emotions and he knew at last he had got through to him.

'I love my job. I need it. If I lose this position I'll end up working for my stepfather and I'd hate it. I love horses not the sea.'

'Then don't threaten others and he'll not find out from me.' Tobias held out a hand. 'Truce?'

The lad smiled and shook Tobias' hand. 'Truce.'

'Truce, sir!'

'Aye, Truce, sir.' Jimmy relaxed a little to his former self. 'Why would you not turn me out after what I just done?'

'I was once cocky and young myself.' He clipped the back of Jimmy's shoulder, 'Now get on with your work before I change my mind.'

'Jane!' Miss Ruddick's voice could be heard across the yard as she approached the laundry building. 'Jane!' The call came ever closer as Chloe straightened her cap, tucked a stray hair into it and appeared at the laundry doorway.

'Yes, ma'am,' she replied.

The woman was visibly flustered. 'What, girl, have you been saying to whom?' Miss Ruddick's anger was almost tangible. She was trying to stay controlled but her body was on the point of shaking with the rage contained within her.

'I don't understand. I have been in the laundry watching over the copper since early. Other than Martha I haven't spoken to a soul.' Chloe wondered what she was supposed to have done now.

'You are the most deceitful, ungrateful girl. I have ever had in my service. You throw yourself into the arms of Mr Poole causing him untold grief and then . . . '

'I have never been in the arms of Mr

Poole or any other. It is a lie!' Chloe spoke out without thinking or choosing her words carefully. The slap she received stung and should have been expected but she was shocked by its sting and struggled not to punch the woman in return.

'You were seen when he carried you to Martha after you fell asleep doing your work! If I'd been there I would have woken you with cold water from the well — that would have taught you to abandon your work. Now you conspire behind my back! Well I hope you end up turning the spit for hours at a time. If you think life is hard in my laundry, you wait until you spend hours over the range in a hot kitchen, or are up making dough for the daily bread. You have not escaped toil, girl, you are about to find out what it is! Scrubbing pots and pans is harder than scrubbing clothes. You'll need to be stronger than you think to survive in there. And may I remind you, that taking one crumb of food from the kitchen is paramount to theft and at the least will result in instant dismissal!' The woman was almost out of breath as she stopped talking and inhaled deeply.

'I don't understand. Am I to work in the kitchen?' Chloe was stifling the rising excitement she felt as it was obvious she was to, but was almost too scared to believe it in case Ruddick was playing out some bitchy jest. But then, staring at the woman, seeing two rosy patches of high colour in her normally sallow cheeks, she knew that her outburst was not driven by humour, not even in a warped sense of the word.

'Collect your things and report to Hebden immediately and stay out of my sight!'

Chloe turned to run back into the laundry and carry out her orders with joy in her heart for once when Miss Ruddick grabbed her arm.

Chloe stared at her hand and then into the woman's eyes.

'Stay away from Mr Poole. He is too good for the likes of you!'

Chloe looked back down at the woman's hand and pulled her arm free. She said nothing in reply but returned to collect her things. He must have arranged this, she thought. That is why Ruddick is so furious and jealous. She smiled, but then remembered the words about her being in his arms.

8

Chloe arrived at the kitchen with her bag in her hand. She was lucky to have belongings to need a bag of her own, but what was neatly folded away in there was her past, and she treasured each and every item within it. It looked too heavy for her to carry, but although Chloe was light of frame she was far from a weakling. She had ridden horses with her father and shot game. Much of her youth would have suited a lad better but she had been out of doors a lot when her father was there to take her.

'So, young lady, I am to be blessed with thee. Should I be honoured? What strings did you pull to make the crossover from laundry to kitchen? In double-quick time too.' Mrs Hebden stepped forward and folded her arms under her bosom. 'I have a feeling I'll have to watch thee, lass.'

'Didn't you ask for me?' Chloe asked, not understanding why and what was going on.

'Innocence becomes you. I am quite tempted to believe you are as green as thee looks. Who wants you in the house, though, that is the question and you'll call me Mrs Hebden or ma'am?' Mrs Hebden waited for a reply.

'I do, Mrs Hebden,' Chloe said honestly.

'Well, unless you have powers you had best not admit to, I would say you either have a protector or an admirer, or both. Which ever it is I would thank you not to bring trouble to my door. That Ruddick woman will think I did this to spite her. I haven't the means or the time to pester with such things. Lass, tread very carefully here. There was a young lass called Betty last year. Now Betty thought her day had come when she left the dampness of the laundry rooms for the warmth of me kitchen and it ended in her ruin. Don't you go the same way. Now, put your things through there.' She pointed to a door which led off from the other side of the kitchen. There was a small room with a cot and a wash stand and a bucket. 'That will be your place for now. Mind, with the baggage you bring we may have to seek a larger accommodation for thee.'

'No, Mrs Hebden, this will do fine.'

The older woman laughed out loud. 'Ee, the nerve of thee and you not even seeing it.' She shook her head. 'You get up first and start the fires burning, water boiling and oven warming. That bit is not so different to what you have been doing, I suppose.'

Chloe put her bag down and, although the room was small and whitewashed, clean and pale, it had a window which looked out over the yard in front of the stables, the bell tower to the left and the grounds beyond. Above her the family had the huge hall to themselves, but here she had her own small space and a view. No Martha to disturb her sleep either. She must remember to thank Mr Poole when next she saw him if it was he who had arranged her place. She could not think that anyone else had unless her father had sent money to the master of the house. She wondered if this were possible. Had he called in a favour and was watching over her from afar? She liked that idea and hoped it was not Mr Poole. She had already put herself in his debt, and she disliked the feeling.

'Stop day-dreaming or I'll shut off the view. You start work now. Did the stick woman let you eat before you came in here?'

Chloe shook her head.

'No work gets done well on an empty stomach. Come hither and I'll see what I have in me pot. Aye, you can have some of yesterday's stew and no wasting it, mind. You eat here what you're given and no complaining, you hears me?'

Chloe nodded that she understood. There'd be no complaining from her, that was for sure. She hadn't eaten a proper meal in the three weeks she had been at the hall. The future, she decided, was looking better, for with a full stomach, she could stop thinking about food and start thinking about how she could escape to a better life with her mother.

Chloe's first week went amazingly quickly. She ate more in that seven days than she had been allowed the previous three weeks. Martha had always taken the most of the food set aside for her, Tilly, Mary and herself.

She had put back a little of her previous weight, which was a relief to her because she did not like feeling her ribs so easily. Even her dress had hung loose on her.

'Jane,' Mrs Hebden's voice called to her. She was still to be called Jane, the family found simple names easier to remember, if they ever needed to speak to the servants, so they took the liberty of renaming all who came. Tilly was really Florence, Mary was Gertrude and even Martha had not escaped being really a Margaret. Only Chloe seemed to take offence at it.

'Yes, Mrs Hebden,' she replied eagerly.

'Here, run over to the stables and give Jimmy this, but be discreet about it. I don't want all the grounds staff pestering me or I'll be in bother for wasting food.' She handed a small bundle wrapped in a piece of the muslin over to Chloe. Chloe took it and slipped out of the kitchen, along the corridor and ran across to the stables, trying to be as unobtrusive as possible.

'Jimmy,' she said softly, as she entered the stables. No reply was heard. She walked inside. This was the nearest that she had been to a horse since she left her home. Their animals had been stabled behind the inn. She walked along looking at one fine animal and then another. Without realising it she had walked to the furthest stall. This was obviously where Jimmy slept. She looked at the neatly made up cot, the threadbare blanket tucked in around the edges. He took pride in his space, as she did hers. Quickly she slipped the small bundle under the pillow and stepped back making sure no sign could be seen of it.

She backed out straight into Tobias.

'Sorry!' she almost jumped away from him.

'What brings you here?' he asked, looking at her as if appraising the reason for her obvious anxiety.

'I had a message from Cook for Jimmy, but I can see he is not here.' She stepped to the side as he walked over to Jimmy's cot.

He bent over and lifted the pillow up slightly with one finger. 'I have seen messages like this before. He is a lucky lad.'

'Please don't tell on her, she means well and he did some work for her.'

He stood straight. 'I am not in the habit of 'telling' on people who are doing someone a good turn.'

'I know . . . I am sorry.' She had been

waiting for an opportunity to speak to him but it was difficult as he was often on the estate and she spent nearly all her time within the hall, below stairs. 'I wanted to speak with you, Mr Poole.'

He tilted his head on one side, intrigued.

'Thank you for helping me when I fell asleep.'

'You are welcome, Chloe. She, Miss Ruddick, was being unfair on you.' He smiled at her.

'And thank you for having me transferred from the laundry to the kitchens.' There she had said it, but could tell instantly that he had not been the one who had done it.

'I would love to accept all your thanks, but I cannot on this because it is beyond my jurisdiction to have done so — much as I would have liked to. Someone else must have taken pity on you.'

His smile had vanished, but hers grew.

'My father must have made the arrangements for me before he was sent away. He never intended me to stay as a laundry maid.'

'Are you sure?' He seemed concerned.

'Who else would?' she shrugged. 'I must go, before I am missed.'

She started to make her way towards the entrance of the stables being careful where she put her feet, when they heard a horse been ridden into the yard. Chloe gasped as she felt his arm close around her waist as he swept her up, almost lifting her off her feet as he swung her back into Jimmy's stall. 'Stay down low, do not come out. It would be very bad for you if you were found in here with me.'

Chloe realised what he was saying was true so she sat quietly on a three-legged stool in the furthest corner, hoping whoever came into the stable would go quickly. She was going to be in Cook's bad books and knew it could be the end of her ever being sent on errands again.

Tobias walked briskly to take the

horse from the master's son who had halted it just outside the stables.

'There you have it! Fine animal. I love a filly with a good head, eh, Poole?' He slapped the horse's neck and slipped down from the saddle.

'Yes, sir.' Tobias took the reins. The horse had been sweating; he had run her hard.

'See that the lad gives her a good seeing to and send word to the kitchens that I require a tray bringing to my room. I am ravenous. Tell Cook to send me something fresh.' He looked up at the clear blue sky. 'Lovely day. Go on, man, set to, Poole, or else I shall faint from lack of food.' He strode around to the main entrance whistling as he went.

Tobias walked the horse in as Chloe appeared from the stall. 'Poor horse, it's been ridden hard. He should take more care of her.' She stroked its head.

'You can't tell a man like that what he should do unless you have him on a battlefield and his life depends upon him listening to you.' There was bitterness to his voice as he spoke, but then he looked back at Chloe. 'You are used to horses? Can you ride?'

'Yes, I love riding, or at least I used to.' She was watching him remove the saddle.

'I should give his message to Cook,' she said, and moved away.

'No, you wait here with Tansy, and I'll pass the message on. When Jimmy returns, which shouldn't be long, you can give him his food.'

'But you heard the master. Mrs Hebden will need someone to take his tray upstairs.'

'Then she will find someone else. You stay here. I shall explain to her why.'

His voice was firm, his manner equally determined as he left. Chloe did as she was told. He was a troubled man, she decided, apparently given to mood swings and acting on impulse, but he would explain to Mrs Hebden his reasons, no doubt, so she happily stayed with the horse as she was told to do, remembering fondly her past.

9

Jimmy waited anxiously until Will arrived the next day.

'Hello, what news have you from town?' he asked, as he ran to meet the wagon.

Will slowed the vehicle almost to a stop, letting him climb up next to him.

'Not a lot. The houses are being built along the new road. The old cottage folk don't like it and say that strange folk will take over the town. They don't like change. Mind there is a family who have moved who have two daughters about our age. I saw one look at me in church. Henry Tillman was in the inn last week, but he was only passing through. I was in and eavesdropped as much as I could as I helped Jethro out. Pa's happy as he is getting lots more work because of the development. What's happening here, Jimmy? I heard the young master has been gambling again heavily. Jethro told me that his cousin runs an inn in Harrogate and he knew of a game where he lost over a hundred guineas. He said the next night he won twenty and celebrated by spending the lot with his friends.'

'Did Henry Tillman say anything about Branton or meet anyone else there?' Jimmy asked.

'Nah, he didn't stay for long and only passed a few moments with Mr Poole, but other than that, no, he was out of there quite quickly.'

Jimmy's eyes widened. 'He spoke to Poole? He knows him?'

'Well, they nodded as if they was acquainted. I believe that they spoke briefly but he didn't drink with him. They were definitely known to each other because he called him Toby. Why? Is there something going on with the laundry lass?' Will looked at Jimmy, clearly hoping there was.

'She isn't a laundry maid anymore. She works in the kitchen now and has settled very comfy in there. The wench even has Betty's old room.' Jimmy looked down at the wheel.

'You miss her, don't you?' Will's voice softened.

'Aye, I miss her. I feel awful, sick to my stomach when I think what could have become of her and the babe; not knowing where she is and what has become of her is awful.' Jimmy glanced at Will. 'I wondered if you could find out for me. I'm not allowed off the estate much.'

'You know people wouldn't talk to her. They sent her over to the workhouse, but she didn't get in there. They said they were full and her with a fat belly meant that she was wanting care for two. They turned her away, Jimmy. I haven't heard where the lass went next.' Will lowered the tone of his voice. 'It wasn't your fault, none of it, you were always a good friend to her.'

'You may choose to see it that way, but no one else would. She should have come to me when she knew she was in trouble. I'd have done something for her to help.' Jimmy flicked a fly away from his waistcoat.

'Like what? Marry her? Who'd marry a lass carrying a babe already? She took a fall when she took a tumble. People would have known that it wasn't yours and she'd be labelled a whore, and you a fool, so that is no way to think. Where would you raise a family, Jimmy? In a stall in a stable? You couldn't move away, you're only a stable lad. Talk sense, Jimmy. She messed up her own life. I'd not let her drag you down with her. I'd have knocked some sense into that skull of yours.' Will spoke with conviction.

'Will, listen, you don't understand, I'll explain when I know where she is. I need to find out, but I can't leave the estate. Can you try?' The wagon reached the yard; Will slowed the pace again as it came through the archway of the bell tower.

Will shook his head. 'You're heading for the asylum, Jimmy. You must be mad to care. But if it will help you to sleep nights then I'll see if I can find out some more at the inn. Perhaps Jethro knows. I'll try. Now has Poole taken to Ruddick yet?' Will's voice was full of excitement again.

Both lads jumped down and Will walked the horse across to the trough. They were lost in their own conversation and failed to notice someone move in the shadows of the tower — someone who had been standing at the edge of the yard.

'No,' Jimmy laughed, 'he'll never do that. He only sweet talks her when he wants something. She's soft on him, but is too stiff around the collar for him.'

'Must be all that starch in her laundry, it's affected her. Have you seen how she stands and walks?' Will and Jimmy started to unload the wagon, laughing and gossiping as they worked.

From the shadows Miss Ruddick retraced her steps from where she had been standing, realising she had forgotten something. Those precious moments whilst she searched her mind for what it was had been opportune. She had listened to the chatter of Jimmy and Will. You always learned things when one listened, but this time she had heard words which stung, burning her pride and piercing her heart. She retraced her steps to her office where she now remembered she had been collecting her keys. She ran back inside and slammed the door shut behind her. They would pay for mocking her. Jimmy would never speak of her like that again, and as for Will, she would think of something. Tobias would be the first to fall. So he laughs at her behind her back, she thought. Her time for revenge would come.

10

Tobias wandered into the kitchen garden, taking three pheasants he had shot as an offering. Yesterday he had brought rabbits in, the day before he had trapped a hare. On each visit he was hoping to see Chloe, but was to be disappointed as this week she had been helping in the dairy. Today, he knew would be different as Cook was visiting her sister this afternoon. The woman lived in the village and was sickening. She had not been well for months. The family had kindly turned a blind eye to Cook's little absences, as she worked so hard and always left plenty of prepared food available for them. The Branton wench intrigued him, he wasn't sure why, but had put it down to a protective streak which lingered within him. Despite all he had seen and experienced in the war, he still believed in innocence and truth. She seemed to represent both, and was attractive and feisty too. He was tempted to turn and walk out. Such thoughts left a man's heart vulnerable and he had sworn he would never be vulnerable again.

* * *

Chloe had only one day free from work again in each month and this was at the discretion of Cook and the family needs. She had not gone anywhere in the first month; instead she had ambled around the estate, amazed that so much land could belong to just one family. Chloe's heart was troubled, her mind restless when she should be sleeping, but at least she didn't lay in the darkness anymore listening to Martha's vibrating throat and feeling the hunger in her stomach. What troubled her now was that she did not have the money needed to travel to see her mother. She needed to have two or three month's pay behind her and then she would be able to. Chloe had worked out that she needed to rent a horse in order to get there and back in a day, otherwise it would be impossible for her to do it. Chloe also acknowledged that even if she could find the horse, it would be dangerous for her to travel on her own, but she worried so much about her mother that, it would surely be worth the risk. If she didn't go, or at least try to find a way she would never know if her mother was suffering. Her father could write and he had taught Chloe, but Ma had refused to learn. She was not a clever woman. She hid from her failings by saying there was no need for a woman to know it and had been too proud to try.

Chloe saw Tobias enter. Happiness swept through her. Why? She smiled at him; it was spontaneous and genuine. Chloe was even surprised at her own reaction, although beneath this a thought crossed her mind. Tobias knew horses and the area. He was strong, well travelled and had proved to her already he had a kindly heart, who had helped her and never pestered for her favour or asked for anything in return. 'Mr Poole, would you like a drink?' she asked, as she had wanted to talk to him for days. Cook had given instructions to the rest of the staff to take a few hours rest as they had worked into the small hours preparing everything needed for today so that she could leave her post for a few hours. Chloe's room was just off from the main kitchen; therefore, she found she had the place mainly to herself.

'Yes, thank you.' He looked around.

'Cook is in the village. Could you take the birds through and leave them to hang?' Chloe asked him.

'Yes, of course. Where are the others?' he asked casually, as he crossed over to the door which led to the store rooms.

'Busy elsewhere. Everyone will be back in an hour or so.' She placed a cup on the table and poured warmed milk into it. Chloe stirred in a spoonful of honey and gestured he should sit down and enjoy the drink with a cut of the morning's bread.

'You spoil me, Chloe. Do you like it better in here?' He seated himself at the table and asked her to join him.

She took down another cup and poured more milk from the jug into it, stirred in the honey and cut herself a slice of bread also and then sat down opposite him. 'This is quite wrong, inappropriate behaviour I think, but forgive my forward behaviour, Mr Poole, as I wanted to speak to you.'

'Really, I wouldn't call two friends sharing a drink together as inappropriate. However, I'm flattered and surprised, or do I flatter myself and should I really be asking what can I do for you?' He grinned and bit into his bread.

'You are correct in your assumptions. But I do need information, I need . . . advice.' She took a genteel bite of her much smaller piece of bread, watching him as he raised an eyebrow.

'What about? I am intrigued.'

'I need to visit my mother, who as you will no doubt have heard is living in a village called Seaham. Next Sunday is my day off. I only have the one so to get there I need to ride. It is too far to walk. I don't know where to find a horse for hire, how much it would be, and how exactly to get to Seaham, only that I must head for the coast and head south a five to ten miles.' Chloe looked at the expression of amusement, or perhaps it was bemusement, cross his face.

'You cannot be seriously considering this. It would be expensive, you would be at best rented a nag and, Chloe, it would be extremely dangerous for you to leave the estate on your own.' He leaned forward, resting both his hands on the table.

'I can ride, quite well actually. I know a nag when I see one. What I don't know is how to get there and who would rent an animal to me. I haven't time to go into the village and arrange this . . . I thought perhaps you might be able to help me.' She stared at him. She thought that as he had helped her before he was her only chance of pulling such a daring scheme together.

'I do not doubt your ability to ride, Chloe. I doubt you would be your father's daughter if you were a fool. I meant that you would not be able to afford a decent animal and no one would rent you one. Also, it is too dangerous an undertaking for you to attempt on your own.' He finished his milk.

'So, what am I supposed to do? Work here till I am an old maid not knowing what fate befell my poor mother? I'd rather walk the distance if that is all the help you can be!' She was vexed and frustrated, knowing he was right and she was wrong did not help her situation. 'Is that all the help you can offer, Mr Poole? I thought we were friends.' She had also leaned forward as she spoke. Her words had poured out from her without censorship. As she realised what she had just said, Chloe coloured. 'I'm sorry, that was unfair of me. You owe me nothing — not even the time of day.'

He cupped her hands in his. 'We are friends, Chloe, but you have to see sense and listen to me. It is possible that there are people out there who work the coast, who knew your father. They have lost much from your father's arrest. They may think they can take it out on you. Take my warning seriously, Chloe, it is not safe for you to leave the hall.'

'Think what my family have lost!' She shook her head. 'If what you say is true then I must see my mother. If they would hurt me, what would they do to her? She is no longer young.'

Tobias still held her hands in his. She could see he was trying to tell her something, reluctantly, he hadn't said it all. But what was it?

'You would be more of a catch for them.'

'Catch? I'm not a fish, Tobias.' She

pulled her hands away, unaware that she had used his given name, and picked up the cups placing them in the sink. He followed her over with their plates.

'You may not be but you are certainly like one who is out of water. This is not your world. I shall find out if your mother is well.' He leaned against the sink and folded his arms, watching her.

'No, thank you for your kindness, but I need to see her. I want to speak to her. We didn't have time to talk properly before we were split up. It is very important, Mr Poole.' She looked up at him.

His deep brown eyes looked into hers and softened. 'I know I will regret this, but ... I will take you. Meet me at dawn at the gate of the estate. I will have a horse ready for you. I will bring a hat and a greatcoat for you to wear. It will be better if you look like a man from a distance, albeit a small one. You will be more comfortable and warmer that way. Can you ride astride, or do you only sit perched on the side of a beast?'

'I can sit astride.'

'Good, meet me at the gate, at dawn on Sunday.' He leaned over and kissed her forehead. 'I hope neither of us regrets this foolish escapade.'

He walked away from her. 'Thank you, Tobias. I can't do it without your help.'

'I know,' he replied, and left.

11

Miss Ruddick watched Tobias leave the kitchens. He was obviously preoccupied, not even aware of her presence. She saw a figure in the doorway — the Branton wench, and Hebden was in the village. So, he had fooled her, he was having an assignation. The lad, Jimmy, had seen right. What a buffoon they must think she is. She strode purposefully across the yard toward him. They will laugh at their own stupidity by the time she had finished with them. She swallowed her pride and approached him.

'Mr Poole, I wondered if I could have your help.'

Tobias looked up at her, forcing a smile. Miss Ruddick could now see his eyes did not reflect the same emotion. He had insulted everything she held dear, her honour, her good name and her belief that he held her in his affections.

'What can I do for you, Miss Ruddick?'

'I need Jimmy's help in the laundry for an afternoon. I have decided to relocate the mangles and possers. I could do with some extra muscle. Do you think you could ask him to come over later?' She smiled, broader and with more confidence than she usually would show him. Miss Ruddick did not lack confidence but had thought it more attractive to a man if she appeared a little less so in their presence. She had realised that Tobias was not the kind of gentleman who would like a woman to be more intelligent or bolder than he. However, as she glanced back towards the kitchen entrance she had not expected him to sink his sights so low as to make a play for a lowly maid — a convict's daughter at that.

'Of course . . . is that all?' he asked.

'Yes, I think so, for now,' she replied,

and waited for him to walk a little way. He seemed eager to be about his business, or was it, she wondered, to be away from her if her feelings towards him had been so publicly and easily read that even Jimmy and Will could see.

She let him believe he had escaped from her presence and then added, 'Cook is in the village, Mr Poole. If you are hungry I could prepare a tray for you.'

'No, that won't be necessary, I was merely delivering pheasant.' He had only paused momentarily before continuing.

'Talking of peasants, Jane seems to have adapted well,' she remarked curtly.

He stopped and faced her, his manner more adamant, slightly challenging. She was starting to annoy him. It pleased her.

'I wasn't talking about peasants, as you know, Miss Ruddick, but I would agree she has. The work suits her better than that of a laundry maid. She is slight of frame and would have been wasted in there.'

'Far better she scrubs pots in a kitchen then. I should think she will please Mrs Hebden as she has the makings of a good little scrubber.'

'Is there anything else, Miss Ruddick? I have work to do.'

'Flighty by nature too, so I have learned . . . and seen. Only the other day she was making eyes at the young master, brazenly talking to him outside the main entrance of the hall. I tell you, Mr Poole, if she doesn't take care she will end up like Betty did. Shame. Gossip spreads like a plague. Still, maids are ten a penny and she has her father's blood to contend with.'

'Good day, Miss Ruddick.' He continued to the stables.

Ruddick grinned. He did not like being toyed with, but dared not confront her. She could see by the look in his eyes that learning Chloe had already caught the young master's eye had hit him hard. It was time the girl did so again, and soon, but how could she arrange it? It was not Miss Ruddick's place to go into the hall, or send a housemaid about her duties there. Somehow she would find a way. Meanwhile, she would start manipulating young Jimmy. Now there was a lad who was ready for a fall. Ruddick genuinely felt happy. She had much to do. There were changes going to happen at the hall and she would be the one who triggered them. No one would treat her as a fool again.

★ ★ ★

Tobias entered the stables, picked up a baling hook, swung it into a bale of hay and threw it into an empty stall. That woman had wised up to him. How he did not know or really care, but in the middle of it all was Chloe. She only thought of her mother and had no inclination as to the trouble she could find herself in. Now he had promised not only to take her there but he was going to use one of the master's horses to accommodate this lunacy. What a bloody mess, and at the crux of it all was a woman — as always.

He was normally a peaceful even-tempered man. However, he hated manipulating and scheming women. He had to admit he had been manipulated willingly by one, by Chloe, flattered that she had turned to him for help rather than take off on her foolish escapade on her own, and then Ruddick had toyed with him.

What was he to do? The young master had his eye on Chloe. He would have to figure a way to take her away from the hall, but how? They may seek her mother out, yet there was no way of finding out what state she would be in when they found her, other than by turning up. Why should he care? Yet he knew he did. The spoilt excuse of a man, the young master, was a gambler, a drunkard and womaniser to boot, who used his position to prey on hapless servants. Betty would have stood no chance of being listened to if she had spoken about him, she must have known it, which was why she left. God help her. Her and Jimmy were so sweet on each other. He had traced her as far as the workhouse but no one knew what had become of her after she was turned away.

'What's wrong, Mr Poole?' Jimmy asked and stepped back quickly as Tobias turned around sharply with the bailing hook still in his hand.

He saw the look of apprehension on Jimmy's face and tossed it to the ground. 'Nothing, lad.'

'If that is nothing, then that bale must have really annoyed you.'

12

Tobias had not slept well. He knew he was going to be at the gate long before he needed to be, but still could not stop himself from dressing and making ready for the journey ahead. Tobias had selected a coat and hat for Chloe the night before. He shook his head. She may slip from sight all together, lost in a mass of material. She was a dainty lady, who should wear the young mistresses riding outfit, but that would have been a step he'd not dare arrange, even if he could. He smiled at the thought; she would look pretty, no doubt. Although slight, he knew she was gutsy.

In the dark he made his way down the steps inside the bell tower from his door to the yard. The laundry lights were still out. There were no signs of life from Miss Ruddick's quarters he was pleased to note. Her change of heart toward him had been unexpected, but was a relief as she was obviously over her infatuation with him. Now he had to watch his back, which he was used to doing anyhow.

He stroked his horse as he entered the stable and then sorted out the blankets, tack and saddles. He had walked quietly to the end stall. Jimmy seemed to be sound asleep. If he wasn't he was paying no attention to what Tobias was doing, which was just as well — what the eye didn't see the mouth could not tell. Jimmy knew the rules.

Chloe was up early on Sunday morning. She wore her warmest skirt and her riding boots. Her blouse and her riding jacket, which matched the quality and colour of the dark blue skirt, were too grand for a serving maid to wear. However, they were hers and had been her favourite riding outfit. Chloe had lost much of her clothes to the slop shop to be sold as seconds in order to make the money up for her mother's journey. Amongst her precious possessions held within her bag from her happier past, Chloe had kept them neat, to remind her what quality felt like, lest she forgot.

Chloe did not need a looking glass to tell her that they suited her slim frame. The colour brought out the depth within her eyes. She spent some time carefully pinning her hair up out of the way. Around her she wrapped a woollen shawl. It would keep the morning mist from chilling her as she walked down the drive. Once satisfied that she was suitably attired for her adventure she placed what money she had within her pocket, pulled on a pair of black kid gloves and made her way out of the kitchens.

She was up before the dairy maids, so carried on uninterrupted across the yard, skirting around the bell tower until she made for the drive. There was no way of hiding from any onlookers as she walked briskly down its length. The dew still clung to the blades of the grass, glistening.

Chloe prayed that Tobias had not forgotten his promise or been out drinking the night before and overslept. She had no idea if he did drink, but it was a possibility, Jimmy did, even though he was young. How she would return to the hall dressed as she was if he was not there and explain herself to Mrs Hebden, she did not know. The realisation hit her that she would probably be returning to be seen in her best outfit, anyway. It might be dark before she returned. Hopefully, everyone would be abed. She dismissed all thoughts of her return, realising that deep down she hoped she would not have to. She really wanted to stay with her mother. That decision was to be made many miles away. Firstly, she had to find her and for that she needed Tobias. Strange how easily she trusted this man.

The legacy of Betty's fall had been dangled about her like a cane to chastise her of the ills of wanton behaviour, or as a carrot to tempt her into temptation. Strange, though, she thought, that everyone seemed to have presumed it was the master whom she had conceived the child with. No one suspected Tobias. The young master had made no attempt to procure her attentions when she had run into him, yet he was supposed to be a letch. Perhaps he liked a different kind of woman — one who was not skinny, as her mother described her.

She could not help the anxious knot gnawing at her; it was where her stomach should be, only she knew it was not an illness. Did she really trust Tobias enough to leave this place without telling anyone where she was going or with whom? She must surely doubt him.

Chloe approached the gates and she saw the movement. To the side, hidden by the trees from the hall's view, were two tethered horses. One was Tobias's and the other the daughter's unused mare. She smiled brightly as Tobias stepped forward from the trunk he had been leaning against. Draped over his arm was a greatcoat, and in his hand he held the broad brimmed hat. Chloe stepped into the shade to meet him. It was then she realised that the knot which had gnawed at her, unravelled, to be replaced with a feeling of joy instead. Chloe was relieved that it was neither fear nor doubt that had caused it, but the excitement of the ride ahead of them . . . just the two of them, Chloe and her friend, Tobias.

13

'Good, you are early,' Tobias held out the coat to her, She noticed he was staring at her outfit. 'It suits you fine. Did Miss Clarissa say you could use it?' He looked at her a little anxiously.

'No, I took it without asking her.' Her reply obviously shocked him.

She giggled, and thought she had better explain before he thought her a thief. 'It is mine, Mr Poole. Do you think it would fit so if it had been made for another person?'

'Pardon my ignorance, ma'am.' He bowed slightly. 'If I'd known you had a wardrobe of your own attire to choose from I would hardly have brought you this old thing.'

Taking the coat from him, she saw the relief in his eyes at her words. 'I see you too are early, sir.'

He grinned. 'I needed to get Miss

Clarissa's horse out of the stables before the maids were up and about. Best to avoid gossip where one can.'

'Did you ask her permission to use it?' Chloe asked cheekily, wrapping the greatcoat about her. The sleeves hung long over her hands. The hem touched the ground and the material was wide enough to have wrapped around her twice. Tobias plonked the hat on her head and the illusion was complete. He was taking a scarecrow for a ride.

'No, I did not. She has not ridden him in six weeks. She hates riding and if it were not for me and Jimmy exercising her regularly she would be perishing in the stable for all the young lady cares.' He seemed vexed. Chloe suspected he did not have a lot of respect for Miss Clarissa.

'You are taking a great risk for me, Tobias.'

He rolled back her sleeves and fixed the chin strap on the hat so that it did not slip from her. Fortunately her thick hair piled atop her head helped to pad the hat out so that it sat on her brow, almost fitting as it was meant.

'We are taking a great risk. If we are found out, Chloe, it is you who will possibly lose your position. Not me. It would be your reputation that would be irretrievably damaged. Do you still want to risk that?' Satisfied that her sleeves were balanced he lifted her up onto the horse's saddle, without pausing or asking her if she needed help. He continued to spread out the skirt of the coat over her legs and the horse's back.

'Thank you, I could have done that myself!' she snapped.

'No, you could not. Not with this on,' he tugged the coat, 'it would have become tangled up.' He mounted his own horse. 'We must leave now.'

'You seem to already know my answer, Tobias.'

'Yes, you are fixed on this lunacy and I must be equally mad to have accommodated it.'

'Why would I lose my position and not you?' she asked indignantly.

'Because, miss, I saved the young master's life, and that is why they gave me the position here — and, also, I am damn good at what I do.' He gestured to the road. 'Should we?'

'So you can do what you like, how you like and to whom?' Chloe walked the horse forward.

'Not quite, but I will be given more room for error than you.' He rode along side her.

'Unlike Betty.' Chloe saw what she thought was a flash of humour in his eyes.

'Betty? You think that I would dishonour a young woman and then throw her to the wolves?' He laughed. 'Are you sure you wish to ride with such a damnable soul?'

'I didn't mean that at all. I meant there had been no tolerance of her 'situation'. Shouldn't we be making haste?' She knew she had coloured. Her doubts had been too transparent and he read her easily.

He held her reins and stopped both

animals from moving on. 'I am not the child's father. I do not need to dally with maids for my pleasure and I would have never turned the girl away. She made that decision herself. Whoever had lain with her, kept quiet as the grave. I was away at market when she left. By the time I returned her trail had gone cold. No one knew where she went after the workhouse turned her away.'

Chloe's cheeks burned. She had never had a man speak so bluntly to her before.

'Don't shy away like a timid rabbit, Chloe Branton. You wanted to know the truth of it, now you have it. Truth is a gift one shares with friends, extend the gift to me, as I have you. Between us, say what you think, and do not repeat what you hear.' He released the reins, 'Now, we shall pick up speed. There is an inn on the moor road where we can take a break in a few hours. Seaham will be a half hour beyond. We shall need to arrive fresh.'

He kicked his horse onwards. Chloe did not know what to say to his outburst but had nodded her consent. She felt the cool air on her face as they rode beyond the grounds of the hall to the open countryside. Feeling the horse's power moving beneath her she felt the prickle of tears on her cheeks — so much she had lost. This was once her lifestyle and her right. Clarissa was a fool to ignore such a fine animal and the freedom it offered.

They had not travelled far before the rain came down. It hit the brim of her hat and ran off. She saw him look back to see if she was fine with it. The expression of joy on her face must have been all too obvious because he nodded at her and then continued to pick up the pace. Chloe was wet, happy and free — for a day at least.

14

Jimmy watched from the stables as Mr Poole took out the young mistress's horse with his own. He thought it was strange because he had not been woken to saddle it or to ride it for him. Why so early? Then Jimmy remembered the conversation with Will. Poole had spoken to Henry Tillman in the inn. Jimmy's heart began to race. He had always known that Poole had an air of confidence about him; cocksure of himself as his father would have said, but now he realised the truth of it. The man was in league with the Tillmans.

Jimmy was about to return to the warmth of his cot when he saw a figure leaving the hall. He took in a deep breath, not believing who he saw. The back of Miss Clarissa stepping lightly across the yard, and then, brazen as she liked, briskly walking down the drive. What was going on? It couldn't be anyone else, not dressed in an outfit like that, but what on earth was she doing? Eloping with him! 'Hell's bells,' he whispered. No wonder he wasn't interested in Ruddick if he was chasing the posh skirt upstairs. He'll pay for this one, there was no mistake in that. He wondered what he should do. Jimmy knew he could go back to sleep, mind his own business and wait for the news to slip out when her absence was discovered. He could casually mention the horses were missing and suggest they had gone for a ride; that would point suspicion Tobias' way, without Jimmy speaking out. Jimmy remembered being dragged in front of Miss Ruddick. His ear almost burned at the memory.

What was she thinking of, though, going out riding so early in the day, when she hated horses? Why hadn't she made him bring the horse to the hall? Jimmy decided it was all very mysterious. He scratched his head, yawned and was about to return to his slumber when he added two things together to make a frightening sum — Henry Tillman and the rumours he had heard about his link to the trade in women. He grabbed his jacket. Was that what had happened to his Betty? Had Poole whisked her away with him when he was supposed to have gone to the market? Furious, Jimmy clenched both fists. No wonder she had disappeared from the workhouse door; Poole must have snapped her up . . . that was it! His poor Betty; he would have married her. She was everything to him, his friend, his future and his lover. If only she had told him she was with his child, they could have sorted it out.

He ran across the yard towards Miss Ruddick's room. She was the only one he dared approach. Surely, he reasoned, the old bag would know what to do.

★　★　★

Chloe ran into the inn behind Tobias. The building was low beamed and quite dark inside. Their coats dripped rain water onto the flagstone floor. He nodded to Chloe for her to take a seat in the corner of a small gloomy room. She sat on the settle. She tried to remember that she was dressed like a man, or at least a boy. There were two other people seated near the window. One was an old man with his dog lying at his feet. The other, a younger man, who smoked a clay pipe, his damp woollen hat clung to his head. He did not seem to care so long as he could suck the pipe and drink his porter. A low flame flickered in a small fire in the hearth. Although it was only minutes, Tobias seemed to leave Chloe too long. She put her hands into the pockets of the coat. She hadn't expected to find anything in them and was surprised to feel something in the right one. It was a small silver flask. Chloe looked over to the serving hatch; Tobias' back was towards her. She placed the flask in her palm and placed it near the candle upon the table top. It had an inscribed name around its neck. Grateful for her father's insistence that she learned to read she saw the inscription, *Lt. T.M. Poole*. She heard coin being placed on the counter and quickly slipped the flask back into the pocket. She watched him carry two tankards of ale in one hand and a plate in the other. Bread and cheese were piled on the plate which he placed between them on the table.

She was so tempted to say, 'Thank you, Lieutenant.' But she decided against it.

'Eat as you would normally. They will not see you for I am too big an obstacle, but keep on your coat and hat — just in case.' His voice was low and hardly audible.

'Why are you hiding me? I am not doing anything wrong. I am only travelling to see my mother.'

'You forget who your father was.' He continued to eat.

'I would never forget that!' she snapped.

'Precisely. You are his daughter. You were not involved in his business dealings. You do not know the murky world of smugglers — nor should you. But he did and he over-stretched his affairs. In short, he made enemies and left debts.' He glanced down at her.

'You seem to know a lot about 'this murky world' . . . Lieutenant,' she whispered.

He stared at her. Chloe felt a slight burst of triumph. She had managed to surprise him.

'Where did you get that nugget of information from? Only the young master has knowledge of my rank, miss. Perhaps you were more involved with your father's doings than I realised.' He put down his food and turned slightly towards her. 'You are in no position to take me for a fool, Chloe. If you want my friendship, as I explained, you need to be truthful with me, and I shall with you.'

118

She slipped the flask from her pocket. He laughed as much at himself for his own gullibility. 'I am becoming forgetful. Give it here.'

He slipped it into his own pocket.

'How then do you know about my father's dealings?' She leaned near to him, adding, 'Be truthful, if you want to have my friendship.'

He whispered into her ear, his breath so warm on her cheeks that she could almost feel the touch of his lips on her skin. 'Because, Chloe, I worked for the Revenue in Kent and traced the trade back to this area. You could say it was my intelligence which produced the trail that regretfully, for your family, led back to your father.'

Her eyes met his, and as she tried to stand he held her arm firmly. 'Do that, Chloe, and we are both lost. You want to see your mother and I want to return to the hall in one piece, knowing you are safely back in your bed. Think before acting rashly. I had no knowledge of you or your family; I was merely doing my job. I am retired from the services. We are being honest are we not? I will protect you as you are an unwitting victim in all of this, as is your mother. So am I also, for I had to leave my home until all can be sorted. They would have killed me if they had traced me back to my family home. So I am here. Know me as a friend, and keep a keen eye for your enemies for you have them, Miss Branton.' He let go of her arm as she relaxed back into the settle.

'He is a good father,' she said.

He nodded, as if not wanting to argue the point, but clearly reserving his own judgement on the subject. 'Eat something and we will go.'

'I'm not hungry,' she answered a little churlishly.

He pushed the plate in front of her and she reluctantly ate her share. She was hungry, but her stomach had knotted itself again. This man who she felt drawn to whenever he was close to her, was responsible for her father being sent away. She mulled over her own thoughts, realising that the knot was caused because she did not want to admit, not even to herself, that it was her father's affairs which had brought his family down. She loved him because he had a reckless, daring streak, and hated him for it too. If he had not been so they would still be together, but poorer for it, no doubt.

15

Jimmy made his way to Miss Ruddick's door. He stood nervously looking at wood in front of him. Slowly he raised his hand ready to knock upon it. His fist was shaking. If he did this there would be hell to pay for Poole if he was right this time, and a thrashing at the very least for him if he was wrong. How could he be wrong, though? He'd seen Miss Clarissa with his own eyes. He had been sure that Poole despised her as a spoilt, pampered child. Had he been covering deeper feelings? Did she hanker for a bit of rough?

However, were his suspicions suffi-cient to warrant telling on them? He leaned against the wall for a moment; indecision eating him up. So, what if they were eloping — as lovers? Had he the right to pass judgement on them and destroy their lives? No, that just didn't feel right. Poole was too confident to skulk off like that; it must be something else, and he was in league with Henry Tillman, which could only mean that he was involved in the trade. Jimmy stood straight, took in a deep breath and knocked on the door. He had to save the young mistress from ruin without the Tillmans hearing he had any involvement. He would rouse Ruddick's suspicions and then leave her to do the rest.

The door opened slightly. He could just make out the shape of a woman in a white cotton nightdress, her hair tied back into a floppy cap. Her pale face added to the impression of an apparition appearing.

'What is it, boy?' a sleepy voice demanded.

'Miss Ruddick, sorry to disturb you, but I don't know what I should do,' he whispered.

'You make no sense, boy. Do you know what hour it is?' Her voice was starting to fill with her usual sharp notes.

'Yes, and that is just the point. Mr Poole left the estate early, with the young mistress's horse.' He swallowed knowing that he had now crossed a line from which he could not return.

The door opened a little wide. She had wrapped an old shawl around her shoulders. 'Why are you telling me this?'

He could see a glint sparkling within her tired eyes. She was interested. He knew that he had picked on the right person. From now on, she would make the decisions as to what should be done. Poole's fate had just been sealed, but Jimmy could not shirk off the deep feeling of regret. He had broken a trust and perhaps ruined a man he respected, but the young miss needed help. Whatever she thought she was doing she was now completely at the mercy of Poole and they would have to act quickly to return her to the hall before news spread of her stupidity.

'Well, at first I thought he must be restless and had taken the animal out to exercise with his own, but then . . . '

'I hardly think that Mr Poole is a horse thief, Jimmy, if that is what your over active imagination has told you.' She half smiled and yawned behind her hand.

'No, not that, or perhaps that as well — I don't know for sure. You see, Miss Ruddick, I saw Miss Clarissa leave the house and make her way down the drive toward the gates.'

'You saw what? Are you certain? Do you realise the severity of what you are saying?' She looked outside to see if there were any signs of others stirring. She was now fully awake and alert.

'Yes, ma'am, which is why I came straight here to you. I don't understand why she should want to ride so early in the day or why the horse wasn't made ready at the mounting block for her. He did not rouse me but saddled them himself, all quiet like.'

'You are certain you saw her?' Her eyes were wide.

Jimmy realised that this news had in

some way pleased her immensely. For a woman who appeared to display few emotions she seemed positively enthralled by his news. 'Who else could it be, Miss Ruddick? She was dressed fine and held herself upright, walking with a sense of purpose.'

'Wait there whilst I dress. This will have to be handled well. Firstly, there must be no mistakes made by us or we shall both be dismissed and ridiculed. We must make sure that Miss Clarissa's bed is empty. Her reputation will be in ruin if word spreads of this. As soon as I have confirmed your words, then I shall have to approach the family directly. This will require tact on a scale beyond your ability.'

The door closed and he waited, each second hanging in the air as his heart beat with greater conviction. He knew what he saw, he knew what he had been told and it all fell into place, so why did he feel something was still not right.

Miss Ruddick opened the door and quickly stepped out carrying a lamp.

'Come with me and wipe those boots before we enter the hall. We are going to see if Clarissa sleeps in her bed, and if she does not we shall inform the mistress straight away. If she does then you have some explaining to do, boy!'

'I saw her. She was no ghost. A ghost wouldn't need a horse, would she?'

He felt a clip across the back of his head. 'Mind your insolent tongue. You are not with Mr Poole now. You will show me respect, or I will teach you a firm lesson to gain it.'

'Yes, Miss Ruddick,' he whispered as they entered the hall and made for the stairs that led from the kitchens to the ground floor. From here they would take another flight of stairs to the upper levels where the bedchambers were. If either were found creeping around by the household staff all hell would break loose, but Ruddick was determined to find the truth of his words. Jimmy prayed he had this right or else he knew not what he would say in his own defence.

16

Despite the rain pouring down from the heavens, Chloe and Tobias continued along the moor road until they found the rougher track which would lead them down to the village of Seaham. Tobias had told Chloe that she would have to be prepared for rugged terrain and inhospitable people. He had added to this comment that the reverse could equally be true.

'How then would my poor mother survive in such a place?' she asked, the rain dripping from her hat's brim onto the saddle in front of her.

'How indeed?' he replied. 'We shall no doubt find out, but Chloe, unless you see your mother first, let me do the talking and you keep that brim tilted downwards. I am glad it is pouring down as you do not look so out of place dressed as you are.'

'Mr Poole, you did not agree to this venture in order to spy on my family, did you?' she asked, as she followed his horse along a trail through a wooded gill. This path was gradually working its way down from the moor road toward the coast following the path of a river that had cut and wound its way through the earth many hundred of years beforehand. The gradient was becoming steeper and she was glad that her horse was sure of hoof.

He stopped his horse, looking back at her over his shoulder. 'You have uncovered my intentions so easily, how bad an intelligence officer I must have been. I will remember never to work for Lord Wellington for sure I would be undone.' He turned to face the front again and moved his horse forward again.

'If I were a man, Lieutenant Poole, I would knock that sarcastic smirk off your handsome face!' Chloe raised her voice loud enough for him to hear, determined not to give in to his taunts, but then as she saw him glance at her again, his eyes lit up and his smile growing, she realised what she had said. Once again, her mouth had spoken before she had composed her words in her mind first. Damn him! she thought.

He nodded. 'I am suitably rebuked . . . and flattered. I am glad you are not a man, for I am very attached to my 'handsome' face,' he chuckled.

'You are incorrigible,' she muttered.

'You, I am delighted to say, are not. You are a breath of fresh air in a cynical world. However, you could be in danger. Please do not speak again until we are sure of our safety. These trees may have eyes and ears. Shh!' He looked ahead of him and continued along the path.

Chloe peered into the trees, but could see nothing other than the woods and the ferns of the undergrowth. She kicked her horse on so that it was closer to Tobias's and continued to watch him, as he casually surveyed all around them as they moved along. He was handsome, and he knew it, so there was no shame in speaking the truth. She assured herself of that and warmed to the thought. He had said they were to be truthful, so why should she not say if she saw him as such. It did not mean she had feelings for his character — which was incorrigible. Her mind then wandered to what he might think about her, before she remembered why they were out in the rain, tracking across the countryside incognito. Her poor mother, whatever had become of her, Chloe decided she would be strong, as she smelt the saltiness in the air. They were nearing the sea, soon she would be with her, and then she would decide if she should return with Tobias.

The thought of watching him leave without her, caused her sadness. What a fix she was in. She had worked ceaselessly for the family for two months, thinking only of escaping to be with her mother again, and here she was realising that her feelings were changing. She watched the broad back of the man in front of her and sighed. What ever would be the use of her having any feelings for the likes of him; he a man of the government and her father a felon. Tobias would not look the side of the street she was on if it had not been for his pity for her, and no doubt, curiosity about her family. Life was, she decided, cruel.

$$\star \quad \star \quad \star$$

Miss Ruddick went first up the stairs. They were hard and cold, no carpets for servants. The difference as they stepped out into the actual house was marked. Lighting the way along the upper landing, she tiptoed along. Jimmy had wanted to go back to the stables and leave her to it, but she insisted he came with her.

'Miss, I should go back ... I shouldn't be up here ... I ... '

'Be quiet you spineless creature,' she snapped back at him in a hardly audible whisper.

Jimmy wasn't even sure if the woman would remember the right door. Miss Ruddick made her way towards the bedchamber door, the one she thought belonged to Miss Clarissa. She had only ever been in this part of the house once, two years since, when a fever had swept through the upper servants' quarters, and desperate measures had been taken letting the lower servants come to their aid. He knew she had enjoyed the change as she had swaggered about the servants' halls as if she were the lady of the house controlling all the staff. As soon as the crisis was over, despite her best attempts to please, she had been returned to her lowly post, more bitter than ever she was before.

'Jimmy, you stay here and let me know if anyone comes,' she whispered as they stood outside the bedchamber doorway

'How will I do that without raising the house?' he mouthed back.

'Just stay here you useless little . . . '

She bit her lip and slipped inside the room.

Jimmy stood for a moment and was about to make a break for the stairs when Miss Ruddick came back out. She almost pushed him back towards the stairwell.

'She's there!' she hissed. 'What game do you play with me, Jimmy McDonald?'

'I'm not playing any! I saw a young woman, dressed well, almost running down the drive. He took the young mistress's horse. I was scared he was taking her to . . . to . . . Who else could it have been?'

She paused for a moment, looking up as if for inspiration, then as if it had arrived she shook his shoulder. 'Jimmy, go down to the kitchens and see if the Branton wench is in her bed. Come to me in my room as soon as you know and tell me if you find her there. I'll decide what to do then. If she has taken the young miss's clothes and horse we'll have her sent to the lock up!'

'What about Mr Poole?' he asked.

'I'll see to him, don't you worry.'

Jimmy couldn't wait to return to the basement, as Poole called the below stairs where the kitchen maids and tweenies worked. He hated being in the austere surroundings of the hall. Jimmy liked simplicity and open air. Living in such a place made him feel jailed. He ran into the kitchen. The fire had not been lit, there was no oven warming. He went to the door opposite and opened it slowly. The bed was made, the uniform was hung on a peg on the wall, but there was no Branton wench. He froze as realisation dawned again. He had been right all along. Poole had tricked the lass; he was delivering her to the Tillmans. He shook his head. The family may not even care, but she would never see this land again if he didn't get her help. He ran out across the yard to report to Miss Ruddick. He felt heavy hearted because he knew she would not give a damn about the lass's fate; she hated Chloe for taking Poole's attention from her. If only she knew how lucky she had been. He ran into her room, but she was not there. Confused as to why she had not yet returned, he waited.

★　★　★

Miss Ruddick had lingered a while longer than she should have. She looked at the ancestors staring down at her from the walls. In the dim light of early morning they looked as if they were rebuking her. She was distracted and tempted by her dreams of ever living in such a fine home. She walked over to the main stairs, feeling the carpet beneath her feet. Her hand traced the polished mahogany hand rail as she slowly made her way down opposite the large doors to the front of the hall. Her back was straight; her head held high, she imagined she was the lady of the grand house. Her name, Amelia, suited the grandeur of the place. She would have arranged balls, trysts, masquerades and so much more

. . . if only her father hadn't gambled, she would never have ended up in such a lowly position in life. At least she would have lived in a respectable town house. The Branton wench was only just starting her years of paying for her father's blunders, yet she had already ensnared Tobias Poole. Jealousy stabbed at her heart. She had been slow to see it, and should have arranged for the young master to see her again. Like the Dolly Mop, Betty before her, she would be ruined.

It was only as she stepped off the bottom stair, her hand on the rounded carved end of the rail, that she realised she was not alone. A hand — a man's hand — covered hers.

She turned to look, and met the young master's stare as he stepped forward from behind the rail. 'Well, well, what do we have here — a servant wench roaming my home looking for what? Or have I discovered a thief?'

'Sir, no, I am no thief.' The panic she felt inside almost made her legs buckle under her. What had she done? 'I can explain, I was looking for you and, I . . . '

She had no chance to finish her sentence as he took hold of her hand and swung her around and into the curve of his arm. 'I think I should make sure and search you. Who knows what you could have snatched whilst my family slept.' She squealed and protested but he silenced her protests with a kiss as he swept her into the shadows. She could taste the brandy still on his lips. She struggled against him. This should not be happening to her. It was the Branton wench he was supposed to want, he was supposed to have. He was strong and she was not. She had neither strength nor position to rebuff him as he dragged her into the library, shutting the doors behind them.

17

The ground levelled out as they approached the beach. The river that had cut its way along the gill as it wound down and out into the open sea. On the edge of the flat sandy beach, the other side of its path, was a cluster of cottages behind an inn which stood defiantly on the edge of the beach. Towering over these was the headland of Stangcliffe. This was Seaham.

'We will head toward the small inn. Remember to stay atop your horse until I ask you to dismount, then, when I say you can, stay silent and tilt the hat down. You can be my simple brother, until such time as I see it is safe for you to be yourself.'

She nodded, but as they approached the back of the inn, a woman came out of the door, wiping her hands upon her apron. She was tall and slim and bore a striking resemblance to Chloe. Before Tobias could speak to her, Chloe swung down from her horse, removed her hat and ran up to the woman. She swung her arms around her, 'Mother!' she exclaimed through the rain, she was wrapped with delight and pure joy. Tobias shook his head as the women stared back up at him, Chloe showing pleasure but her mother's concern was obvious.

He jumped down from his horse, pulled her back a step from the shocked woman and plonked the hat back over Chloe's head. Her mother took hold of her arm and pulled her into the shadows of the small shelter at the back of the inn, which offered temporary stabling for the horses, belonging to any travellers.

The marks on the flat sand told Tobias that most of the fishing boats were out at sea. Thank God for small mercies, he thought, as this headstrong naive fool had acted so rashly. Tobias secured the horses as the two women exchanged further, more subdued, greetings.

'Good heavens, girl. What did you think you were doing coming here?' she looked at Tobias as she tenderly stroked the cheek of her daughter.

'I had to see you, Mother. I had to know you were well. I brought you some money.' Chloe put her hand in her pocket.

'Put that away. I am not short for a few pennies. Do you think your father would leave me with nothing? Did you not get your father's letter?' Her mother still looked bemused.

'What letter?' Chloe asked.

'I told him not to trust the blacksmith! I bet he burned it. Rash, stupid man he is at times. You were to stay at the hall and work until he could arrange for us to move on. You would be safe there. He has friends in all ranks, child. All you had to do was blend in. He paid the man good coin to deliver it.' She peeped around looking at the inn. No one stirred, so she looked a little less anxious.

'I brought money, Mother. I can stay here and help with the work.'

'You don't listen — like your father, I don't need money, I am clean, safe, well fed and amongst friends.'

Her mother was staring at Tobias who was leaning against the frame of the shelter watching both the path through the gill and shore.

'Who is he?' she asked, a sharp tone in her voice.

'He is the estate keeper. He arranged the horse for me and brought me here safely. Mr Poole is my friend.' Chloe flushed a little, despite herself. She felt as though she should say that he is a lieutenant and worked casually for the government, but how could she break his trust and scare her mother, not to mention admit how foolhardy she was.

'If he lays one hand you, Chloe, your father will track him down and . . . '

'I hate to interrupt, ladies, but your husband is in no position to do any such thing. Are you well? Should we leave?' He was being abrupt, but his senses which had kept him safe in the Peninsular were telling him trouble was not far away.

Her mother stepped forward. 'You, sir, fool no one. I can smell a uniform a mile off, and if I can so easily, so will the folk around here. You best take her back safe. My man will collect her as soon as he is able. Meanwhile, I stay here.' She had set herself against him. 'Chloe, pick your friends more wisely in future and do not parade yourself around the countryside with young men. You must have lost leave of your senses.'

'Mr Poole has been very kind to me and is a 'real' gentleman.' Chloe stopped as her mother faced her.

'Mr Poole is using you, girl. You are a fool to think a gentleman would help the likes of you, unless he was helping himself first. I am fine. Your father saw to that and he will collect his lass as soon as he is able. All you have to do is stay put, keep yourself nice, and wait.

Patience never was your strong point, was it, Chloe?'

'Agnes, Amos is looking for thee . . . ' A maid ran around the inn to find her. She stopped when she saw Tobias. He stood straight.

'Betty?' he walked over to her.

'I ain't going back, you can't make me. I took nothing that wasn't mine, the young master gave me the money. I ain't a thief and my bairn's my own.' She stepped back a pace.

'I am not here to take you back. I am relieved you are well. The young master doesn't want to claim his child, Betty. If he gave you money then he has washed his hands of you. I'm sorry.'

'No, you got it wrong. He has been a good friend. He doesn't mean me any harm. It's that Jimmy I had to get away from. He put the bairn there, but how would he be able to care for it? Besides, we were tipsy, it was Christmas Eve, it were a big mistake, but he wouldn't leave me be and the young master found me crying. He got me away. I was

144

nearly in the work house, but bless him, the young master had been drinking and he found me. He is a good man. Sorry, you have been sent on a fool's errand, sir, but please tell them I found a home, but don't say where. I don't want Jimmy coming here. He's no good. He is always dreaming, not working, what good is a man like that?'

Tobias nodded. 'Very well.'

She looked at Chloe's mother. 'You best go back to the oven. Amos is worried for his bread.'

She nodded, and the maid returned inside. Tobias collected the horses' reins.

'Mother, I can't just go back. You need me here and I need to keep you safe . . . '

Agnes put both her hands on her daughter's shoulders. 'Chloe, I love you dearly, but I wish you were less like your father. You're rash and that makes you dangerous. You have got to leave here. I am not your mother here. I am waiting for a message. Until then,

145

I am Amos' cousin and he is giving a widow a temporary home. Now leave and learn patience. You could no more look after me when you can't even see yourself safe.' She turned to Tobias. 'Listen, soldier — whatever you are — don't underestimate my husband's reach. You hurt or harm her in any way and you'll deeply regret it! Now leave.'

She walked into the inn without looking back. Chloe was stunned. She had never had the rapport with her mother which she had had with her father, but she had never been rebuked and rejected in such a way before. Somehow the phrase, 'poor mother', didn't ring true any more. It was as if she had seen her as a different woman, free of her cage of respectability. So how respectable was her father? It was as if her life was a lie. They had played roles within the strictures of a town, when both had lived a much different life.

'Well, are you going to climb up or do you want lifting?'

Chloe swung her leg up but the coat was heavy and she could not lift it high enough. He swept her up on it with little effort. She nodded an acknowledgement but, just at that moment, no words would form.

18

'Sir, I don't know what you think I am, but I am not going to put up with any . . . any . . . ' Miss Ruddick was looking around anxiously avoiding eye contact with him as she searched for her word.

He had pushed her back into the chair opposite the door without using excess force, but with enough firmness to make her sit down. Standing with his arms folded he watched as she sat bolt upright arranging her skirt, to regain her modesty. He had wanted to shock her, and he had.

'Any?' He looked at her through a slight haze of brandy. He was used to drinking and knew he would start to sober up soon. His senses, however, were dulled, but not dimmed completely.

'Any nonsense!' she snapped indignantly.

He leaned forward with a hand on each of the arms of her chair. His face was only inches from hers; she either had to let them touch or shrink back into the chair. She had a sharp tongue, he knew. He had talked to Tobias about her before. 'I shall not stand for any nonsense either, Amelia Ruddick. Ah, I have surprised you. You do not think I know who lives under my own roof. You think me a fool, woman. How little the lowly chamber maid thinks of her master. I suppose you expect me to ravage you here and now. Do you think you are desirable to me or do you think I do not care so long as you are here and I can prey on a defenceless woman?' He stopped himself from saying anything further as he was aware that the alcohol was heightening his senses — he was finding her attractive. He liked her.

Her face coloured. She shook her head. 'I do not want to end up a Dolly Mop, like Betty!' Her voice was breaking. He had scared her and he had not really intended to go that far, just intimidate a little, because she had overstepped her place.

'Betty was no whore, woman, just a foolish girl who should have said no and meant it more. So the rumour that I am responsible for the girl's situation runs wild even in my own home. By the gods, I should have you all flogged and turned out for the insult you do me. No, woman, it was not me or Tobias who was to blame,' he explained, and saw her register the familiarity with which he used his friend's Christian name instead of the usual reference to his surname.

'Then whom?' she asked.

'Ruddick, what do you think you were doing here in the hall? Why were you walking down the stairs as if you owned my home? Why should I not turn you out onto the streets this instance for your insolent behaviour?'

He watched her face dissolve from prim spinster to that of almost a babbling child as she explained what

Jimmy had told her. He listened, he watched, and then he repeated one word. 'Jimmy!'

'Yes, the boy was concerned. He came to me for help and I needed to make sure it was Miss Clarissa who he had seen before I raised anyone's suspicions further. I realise the total humiliation that would be caused to the family if she had acted so recklessly as to have an assignation with a hired hand.'

He considered her words. They were charged with emotion. 'You acted correctly.' He leaned closer to her. 'So why were you dallying on the main staircase, when you knew that it was not her, and should have returned below stairs?'

She looked up into his eyes and swallowed before admitting to him, 'I forgot myself — momentarily. I allowed myself to think . . . to imagine, just for a few seconds that I was better than just a chambermaid. It would never happen again, I swear.'

'I could make certain of that, Amelia.' He kissed her gently on the lips and was surprised when she did not immediately pull away from his touch. 'So you wish to improve your position in life.'

She nodded, obviously warily, not sure what he was asking of her, neither really was he, but he had seen her in a different light as she walked elegantly down those stairs. She had grace, presence and knew how to hold herself aloof. What was more, as her breathing deepened he could tell that beneath the dull fabric of her uniform there was a comely woman.

'Did the boy make the story up? If he did I'll thrash him myself.' He focused on the matter in hand whilst he gathered his thoughts and perceptions. Her eyes were so pale a blue they were almost silvery in the half light from the lamp.

She shook her head. 'I do not believe so. I think he saw Chloe Branton — I mean 'Jane' — leave for a tryst with Mr

Poole.' She stared directly at him as she made this insinuation.

He noted the sparkle in her eyes; she was jealous and had obviously held a desire for Tobias. She was not his social equal. He knew that, he had been ill used by a sophisticated lady in Portugal and would not cross ones path again. The memory made him smile. Until the moment a woman stole Tobias' heart and toyed with it before breaking it into a million parts, the man had been very cavalier with the fairer sex. Tobias grew up overnight. He worked and scoured the country for Wellington's information instead. Money and frippery lost its fascination and Tobias became an honourable man — even to a point now where he was happy to stay as a glorified game keeper instead of returning to his own, smaller but affluent, estate. The woman was fidgeting.

'You do mean the Branton girl. She should not be leaving this estate even if it is her free day. Damn, Tobias, he should have checked with me first.' He turned away. 'Jimmy knows this?'

'Yes, I sent him to see if the girl was still abed or if she had run off.'

'Damnation!' He ran his hands through his hair.

'Tell Jimmy to saddle my horse, I shall have to change and find them,' he ordered, he would have to follow their trail and see if the Tillmans had wind of the girl's adventure. If they did, Jo Branton's fears for his daughter could be realised. He had been paid well to keep her hidden in the hall until her father sent for her. He hadn't told Tobias all the details concerning the arrangement because the less he knew the better. The man was honourable and had now worked for the Revenue. In his innocence he had nearly cost his friend a deal of money and embarrassment had his name been discovered. He shook his head; he had nearly brought them to his own door. Damn his bad luck at the tables. If he hadn't needed the money to clear down his debts before his father heard of them and threatened again to disinherit him, he would never have become involved with Branton, but he had to acknowledge that he was a gentleman in comparison to the Tillmans.

Miss Ruddick quickly stood up, anxious to make an escape from his presence, but he stopped her by wrapping an arm around her waist and drawing her in to his body. 'Listen, Miss Amelia Ruddick, I shall only ask you this once. I know you were from decent stock. Your father was an acquaintance of my father's. If you want to have a more commodious life again, than the one you have now, I can make one available for you.'

'What price, sir, would I pay for this new life style?' she asked looking him straight in the eye, but again she did not pull away from his grip.

'You would be, if you will consent willingly, my lover.'

He felt her breathe quickly, her body betraying her excitement or fear, even though her face remained controlled, he knew he had surprised her. 'I would find you a pleasant cottage on the outskirts of town, and see that all your needs were reasonably met and that you were comfortable. I would take you to town when I go — that's London I refer to, not Gorebeck — and you would be at my convenience, my personal companion when I required company. I would never marry you. I would never treat you ill and if you were good to me, I would be true to you until I needed to wed a suitable bride to provide heirs for the estate. If you put your pride to one side, your life could be one of much amusement, new experiences and thrills, Miss Amelia Ruddick.' He let her go. 'Or you can return to doing my dirty laundry and sleep alone in your small and lonely room. The choice is yours. Think on it until Friday. Give me your answer after dinner, the offer will never be made again, and you will never be able to approach me as an equal again. You would be back in your place until you met a delivery man or died a serving spinster.' He kissed her full on the mouth and was surprised when for a few moments she responded. It was he who pulled away. 'Now go and see, Jimmy. We will talk again on Friday.'

'What, sir, if I should not please you?' she asked calmly.

'I would send you off with thirty guineas in your pocket and a reference for a position as a housekeeper, and you would be free to leave.'

'I would need a maid of all work,' she added.

'Lady, servants talk, as well you know. She would have to be there when I was not. You would sort out those arrangements from a limited fund. Make no more assertions. I have given you a proposition, think on it, and do not stretch it further; it is as it is . . . no more . . . no less.' With a cursory nod he dismissed her, and she left, the servant once more.

He watched her go, Amelia could be a very interesting companion, but he wondered how fickle that pride of hers was. Well, like any good filly you needed to know the bloodline, and hers was suitable for a mistress, but not for a wife. If she turned him aside, she would find her workload would keep her busier so she had less time available to trespass on his stairs fancying herself a 'lady'. He laughed aloud and then he sighed. That boy created so many problems. What to do with Jimmy?

19

Tobias took them back by a slightly different route. He followed the road further around the bay to the slightly larger town of Ebton. From here he led them down a track to an open road to the moors.

Chloe brought her horse forward so that she was riding alongside Tobias.

'I'm sorry, Chloe. I should have refused to bring you here. I suspected that your mother might well be angered by your unannounced visit.'

'Why should you be sorry? I now know she is well, which is what I set out to establish, so we have succeeded in our mission.' She tried to smile reassuringly at him.

His expression was one of open sympathy, which had the unnerving effect of making her eyes water.

'Don't look at me that way!' she said

quickly. She was determined to be strong. She had to be, she had no one else to care for her . . . except Tobias. Chloe dismissed the notion as he had no reason to become involved in her problems. She was on her own.

'Why? You have been hurt, have you not? It was not the warm welcome you craved for that you received. You don't need to hide your disappointment from me. Hurt happens to us all at some point, usually when we least expect it, but it fades.' He looked ahead of them, staring, she suspected, into his own past.

'You speak as if you are familiar with it. Who hurt your heart, Lieutenant Poole?' Chloe saw his eyes widen as she had obviously touched a sensitive point.

'A woman, but not my mother, for she is a dear lady. I think you and her would find you held many views in common.' He glanced back at her.

'I would love to meet her. Does she live locally? I still have an afternoon free; we could visit your mother as well as mine, couldn't we? Would she welcome a surprise visit?' She warmed easily to the idea. Now she had his full attention, Chloe would love to know more about this man's family; she certainly had had enough of her own.

'I think not. Even if we could go straight there and take the packet from Whitby to London, we would still need another day's travel before we would arrive at my home, which is an old manor house. So, I am afraid today we cannot pay our respects to my mother.'

She pulled the reins close to her, bringing the horse to a stop. 'You are from a manor house, Lieutenant Poole? Are you the son of a groundsman or is it possible you hold yourself so well because you are a gentleman? I mean a real 'gentleman' as opposed to just a man who has had some education, honour and manners?'

He scratched his neck with one damp finger; the rain had stopped but they were far from dried out.

'Yes, I suppose I am, but not as rich

or as well positioned as Timothy — the young master — as you all call him, is.'

'Then, I apologise, as I did not mean to be so presumptuous. Of course I would have nothing in common with your mother.' She kicked the horse on. 'We should get back.' Chloe did not look at him as her emotions were already raw, she had no wish to add more embarrassment to her growing sense of gloom.

He rode his mount past her and brought it around to approach hers head to head. Tobias took hold of her reins when he was adjacent to her. Facing Chloe, he asked her two simple questions. 'Did I miss something in our conversation? Was there a comment made which offended you?'

'Not at all, sir. I just think we should return to the hall, that is all.' She was fighting to control the hurt she had felt as her mother rejected her presence, and then learning that Poole was not just slightly beyond her reach, but they were a class or more apart. This had compounded her sense of emptiness. All she had to look forward to now was one of her father's hollow promises as she toiled and aged in the bowels of a rich man's home.

'I think we should not. I think we should find an area of open ground, perhaps a sandy bay and let these animals have their heads. I think we should ride with the wind and let it blow the cares from our minds. Then, I think, we should collapse amidst the dunes, whilst our horses drink from the stream that crosses the marshes and there we should eat the food I brought from the kitchens. Then, and only then, I think we should talk, laugh and enjoy each other's company and what is left of the day, before we return late and unnoticed to the estate.'

She had hung on his every word. With each sentence presenting an irresistible image of freedom, she could not help but smile back at him. 'Would your mother approve of such behaviour

— especially with a lowly maid?' she asked coyly.

'Would yours agree to you behaving in such a manner with a gentleman?' he retorted.

She shook her head.

'Good!' He led her horse around his so they faced back towards the beach and trotted down onto the damp sands. The tide was on the turn, the waves breaking noisily, producing a constant hum. Birds kwaarked and boats could just be seen upon the waves in the distance. Chloe loved what she saw. Far from the confines of the hall's kitchens or laundry this vast expanse represented freedom.

Their trot soon became a canter, which turned into a gallop. With the wind in their faces, the speed and feel of the animal under her as they traversed the bay, she rode like she never wanted to stop. Her hat fell onto her back. The hair she had so neatly piled upon her head unravelled into a wild mane and her joy felt complete.

Freedom was hers for those few precious moments. Only when the village of Ebton was behind them, and they were flanked by the sea to their right and the dunes and marshes to their left, did he slow the pace back to a canter, then a trot until they walked the animals up a path between the dunes to a pool by the marshes. Here he dismounted and led his horse to the water, turning to encircle her waist with his hands, easing her and the greatcoat she was wearing off the horse's back. She slipped down in front of him.

Both of them were in high spirits, their senses alive and heightened. He took off his own greatcoat and spread it on the soft sand. Then he helped her to unfasten hers and swirled it like a cape so that it spread out over his, There was something in the act which he did in silence that made what happened next almost inevitable. He picked her up in his arms and laid her down on top of them. Sheltered from the wind by the mounds of sand held together by the wild marram, he held her in his arms and kissed her lips tenderly. Chloe wrapped her arms around his torso, pulling him to her. She wanted to be held and loved.

She missed the contact that families bring and take for granted. Welcome hugs, pats on the back, even the rebukes and then the making up. All was human contact; she had pined for it until her body ached with loneliness. Chloe was a warm person, she loved, she was not a workhorse to spend her life with tasks and chores, orders and rebukes with no love. Tobias was, she realised, loving her. At first she had been so swept up with the exhilaration of the ride she had fallen into his embrace easily, wanting — and demanding more. The passion she felt was new and exciting, the emotions surging in her like the tide. He kissed her neck and she let him. Chloe lay gazing at the clouds passing above her, then closed her eyes sensing and savouring his touch, it was only when a sharp wind managed to breach their place of shelter that she felt its chill on her breast. Chloe realised he had undone her blouse; his kisses had travelled further than she had intended. She opened her eyes and gasped. His mouth found hers again and his hand now caressed her where his lips had been. Through the desire and her own shameless wanton feelings, stirred a feeling of panic. She had to stop him going further, but as she moved to try to wriggle from under him her movements only seemed to make things worse — or better.

'Tobias!' she managed to say when his lips found her neck again, 'Please, stop.'

He lingered over one last kiss and then slumped to the side of her looking at her exposed flesh. 'You are beautiful, Chloe.' He stood up.

They both rearranged their garments, and as she fumbled nervously with her buttons he produced a package from his saddle bags, which contained their food, and his flask in which he had poured fine wine.

Chloe's colour, like her emotions was high. She was almost shaking with sensations she could not explain. If she claimed it was rage, she would be lying. If she claimed it was disappointment — that too would be a lie.

'We both needed that, Chloe. Don't feel bad about it or shamed. You are not like Betty. I would not have gone further. You must trust me and learn to enjoy life's gifts whilst you can.' He started to eat, so confident was he in knowing what he was doing.

'You do not know what I want,' she said, and took a small bite of the fresh bread, sipping the shared flask of wine.

'Yes, I do, Chloe, but it sits well with me, because I like you too. I think we should step out together. I would like you to consider knowing me better.' He continued to eat.

'I have never given you any reason to believe that I have any affections or desires for you, so why would you presume to treat me so, unless you presume I am a . . . ?' Her focus stayed on the bread. Although her words were brave her confidence was not there to back it up.

He rolled over so that his head was balanced in his hands as he looked up at her. 'Let me see. Where shall I begin, Miss Branton? Because you would not have set foot out of that estate if you had not trusted me . . . Because you came to me for help . . . Because you like my handsome face and because you melted in my arms when they encircled you . . . Because your joy was so complete you did not even realise I had started to undress you . . . ' he laughed, as she raised her hand to wipe the smirk from his handsome face, and then he continued to roll down the slope of the dune.

What could she say in her own defence? Nothing really; he was right in all his statements. She ran down the soft sand after him, his arms were ready for her and he swung her round full circle only stopping to hold her close to him.

'You are incorrigible, Mr Poole.' She laid her head on his chest.

He patted her back. 'And you are going to stay with me. You may still be in danger, Chloe, and I don't mean from your own desires.' He nodded to the beach. Men were running from Ebton across the sands to meet a boat coming ashore. 'Come, Chloe, we must move quickly. We will discuss our future together when we are safe.' Leading her by the hand they returned to the horses, packed up and remounted. He insisted they skirted the marshes behind the dunes in silence and made their way back to the moor road.

The roar of the tide had been replaced in Chloe's ears by the sound of her own pounding heart, and she considered what they had done.

20

Miss Amelia Ruddick gave the message to Jimmy who immediately saddled the young master's horse and took it to the riding block.

'You, lad,' he snapped at a very anxious Jimmy, 'should feel my crop on your back for the trouble you cause people. I will find Miss Branton before any of your stepfather's lot. No, don't you look so surprised. Why do you think I have you here, other than to keep a good eye on what you are up to? One more step out of line and you will be serving on a man-of-war. When we are returned safely to the hall, you shall admit to the whole of the workforce, in the servants' hall, that it was you who defiled the young woman, Betty.' His rage made his voice waver as he mounted his horse.

'But they will hate me for it, and that

is unfair for I tried to find her, honest.'
Jimmy was holding the reins keeping
the horse steady.

'Honesty is not a word that sits well
with you. Yes, they will hate you and the
young girls will be wary of you, which is
no bad thing because you act like an
animal. However, you will survive. You
could not find Betty because she did
not wish to be found by such a wastrel
as yourself. Now do your work and
don't send word to any of your Tillman
relatives, or I'll keep good my word and
you would be better occupied if you
learned to sing sea shanties.'

He galloped down the drive. Jimmy
hated him, even slightly more than he
did himself for abusing and losing his
first love, Betty.

* * *

Miss Ruddick went to her room and
slammed the door shut. So he thought
she would make a good mistress! 'If'
she pleased him, 'if' he would treat her

well — like a good dog perhaps, that should be grateful to a generous master. She seated herself for a moment and thought. She needed to write him a letter. Show him she was no imbecile. Yet, as she looked around at the sparse room, her spare uniform hanging on the hook, she hated everything she saw. Would it be such a trade off? Her 'honour' for what it was worth in exchange for the numerous comforts he could provide. She could live the life, fool herself into thinking she was being as a respectable lady would act if she was actually married to the man; being taken to town — wined, dined and then . . . She stood up. This was no good. She was like a fly caught in a spider's web. She was repulsed by his touch, or should be, but could she honestly say she had been? Her pride had been dented yet again, by a man.

No, she would not have him on his terms; she would write him a letter and explain what she thought of his offer, set out her own, or leave. At the same time she would write her own reference on the family letter paper and go where no one would have heard of them. Yes, she would escape and he had given her the notion of how to do so with honour. She picked up her bunch of keys and locked her door. She would start opening the laundry as usual, but then as the young master left the hall she would slip into the study and use his paper. She would return the note to him later.

Her heart pounded as she entered the room. The desk was large and took pride of place in front of a mahogany panelled wall. The Turkish carpet in front looked almost regal with its warm red colours. She tiptoed over to the desk and saw the headed paper by the ink stand.

She seated herself in the chair, her skin almost tingling with the excitement and daring of what she was doing. Then she saw that the desk drawer had been left slightly ajar. Curiosity was both a blessing and a curse. If it was rewarded with answers then it was a blessing. However, if it was rewarded with being found with ones fingers in a place they did not belong, it would be a definite curse. She wasted no time and ferreted through the papers in the top two drawers — nothing of note there. But then she clicked the fastening for the one shallow drawer which was hidden in the edge of the desk facing its owner. How sweet, she thought, it was like her father's. In here were more private letters, some signed by Mr Branton, Chloe's father. She removed two of note; One giving specific instructions as to how he was to look after the wench, Chloe, along with a list of payments to be made to him via Henry Tillman, to be collected at the inn, for services rendered. The other letter showed that he had been in receipt of goods from Henry Tillman. How stupid the man was to have kept them. She smiled. Now she had him. They would talk about an arrangement, but it was one that would see her father released from the debtor's gaol in York. It would see them living in a cottage on the estate, and it would release her from toil. Young mister Timothy was about to lose the opportunity of having a mistress at his whim, and instead, find he had a new governess. Amelia Ruddick smiled, genuinely feeling happy for the first time in three and a half long years of servitude. She took up the quill, dipped it in the ink, and began to write.

Dear Timothy,

I have stumbled across some revealing letters, which are currently being held in a place of safety on my behalf. I think they may be of interest to you as they concern your account at the 'Tillmans' Bank' — a rather sweet name, which could have so many embarrassing repercussions for you and your dear family should they become public knowledge. I have considered your generous offer for my future and have decided that I am not certain that you would live up to my expectations, so I have outlined my own offer to you below . . . . .

She liked that, and proceeded to state how he was to pay her father's debtors and accommodate her father and herself near to the town. She did not want to appear too greedy. She had also decided to include the possibility of being his guest in town once her father was safe. Time would decide upon other issues.

Of course, I would not expect you to agree without considering your options first. Therefore, I shall expect you to give me your answer by Friday before dinner. I shall be waiting in York for my father's release. If you do not arrange this by that time, the letters will be handed to the authorities there and detailed in the broadsheets. Then you would have the opportunity to become acquainted with my dear father in his present accommodation.

I will do you the same courtesy you

showed me by not repeating this offer to you again.

Yours . . . . . .

She blotted it, folded and sealed it, using his own wax seal then left it on the silver salver on the hall table before slipping out through the kitchens.

'Good day, Mrs Hebden,' she said brightly, as she passed the woman who stood, her mouth gaping open, as Miss Ruddick breezed confidently by.

She shouted to the lad, 'Jimmy, make the gig ready. You are going to take me to town.' She breathed in deeply as if it was the first time she had appreciated the country air.

'Pardon, Miss Ruddick?' He stared at her as she bustled into her room, almost throwing things into her bag. 'I don't think I can,' he said, as he stared at her.

'Yes, you can and you will. What is more, my boy, I will have need of a servant lad in the near future so do this for me now and you too shall escape from this hell hole, as I am.'

'Yes, ma'am.' Without question he ran to the stables to make ready the gig.

★   ★   ★

Tobias and Chloe were half way across the moor road making good progress when Timothy came into view. He was joining the road by the junction where the dale joined the moor road. Two riders, both armed, were also approaching the junction.

'Are they highwaymen, Tobias?' Chloe asked, as his hand slipped inside the saddle and removed a pistol. He paused briefly to load it.

'Stay behind me, Chloe.' If trouble breaks out make all haste to return to the estate. 'I should have brought my rifle with me.'

Chloe watched as the two figures flanked the young master. They were looking over toward her and Tobias.

Tobias kept the pistol in his hand as he approached, but it was not obvious as he held it just above the reins which were gripped firmly by his other hand.

'Henry,' Tobias said acknowledging the older rider, as he stopped still a good ten feet off.

'What do you have there?' the man asked, glancing at Chloe's figure.

She was wearing the coat and hat which Tobias had provided, but had forgotten to tuck her hair back up. Instead, it cascaded freely over the collar.

Tobias glanced at her, 'My betrothed,' he said.

That caused the young master to laugh out loud and Chloe's head to shoot up. She realised how much Tobias was a man who knew his own mind even if he had forgotten to consult hers.

Henry Tillman brought his horse a little closer. Tobias lifted the pistol pointing it at the man's chest

'We are not in Portugal now, Tobias,' Timothy reminded him.

'I know that, Timothy,' he said abruptly, 'What interest do you have in Miss Branton, my fiancée? I fail to understand.' He fixed his attention on Henry ignoring the young master's words.

'Her father cost me dear.' The man glared at her. 'She can repay some — in kind.'

'That is not her concern,' Tobias stated. 'Her father pays you regularly what he owes, when he sends funds to the hall. Don't deny it. It was agreed. Does the Tillman name mean nothing — does their word not stand for anything?' His voice held steady like his gun hand.

'Aye, he pays his coin, but what about the trade we lost when he closed his side down. What about all the money we was to make? I would only take what he cost us. If you've claimed the lass, then I'll take information — she must know where he kept his stash.' The man leered at Chloe.

Tobias' finger curled around the trigger of the gun. Chloe sat silently watching, wondering if she was going to witness a shooting, or as she watched

Tillman's nervous friend, a bloodbath.

'She didn't even know what her father was involved in, so why would she know that?' Tobias replied honestly.

'Are you sure?' the man growled. 'I could find out for sure if you've no mind for it?' he offered, an evil look crossing his face.

'I'm certain. I told you she is my betrothed. Forget your greed. Keep the money for her keep as it comes in. Timothy will have no need of it from now on. I shall be providing for her.'

Timothy rode forward, 'That is not for you to say. I need it!'

'No you don't! It's money you should never have touched,' Tobias rounded on his friend, then as Henry moved his hand on his horse's reins Tobias retrained the gun to point at his head. 'Go back to your homes and be grateful that you still can, and leave her alone, she is with me now!'

Henry Tillman nodded. 'I will, but take my advice, you go far away from here because I don't want to see you or your woman in these parts again.' He nodded at Chloe. 'Good day, miss.' He rode away, his friend following in his wake.

Tobias made the gun safe and replaced it in his pocket.

'You are fortunate, my friend, he believes you,' Timothy said. 'You have cost me dear. I had plans for that money.'

'He is a good judge of character then, because it is the truth. Stop gambling and you won't.' Tobias said with an accusatory note in his voice. Timothy just shrugged.

'What is a man to do?'

'Work!' Chloe said. Timothy laughed and Tobias glanced at her.

'Do you know if he is dabbling in the white flesh trade?' Tobias asked Timothy.

'Hell no! He isn't that big a fish in the pond. Who has been feeding you that nonsense? Oh, don't tell me — Jimmy!'

Tobias nodded. 'What nonsense is

this, that she is your 'betrothed'?' He was laughing at them openly.

'I proposed to her on the beach and she said yes.' He looked at her sheepishly.

'I bet she did. Why not make her your mistress, that's what I'm doing with Miss Amelia Ruddick. I've given her an offer she won't turn away in a hurry.' He laughed again.

'Are you sure?' Tobias said.

Chloe could see that he was genuinely surprised at this revelation.

'Positive, I know how to handle people, Tobias, unlike you. Stop this nonsense and have your fun whilst you still enjoy it. Time enough for marriage when you have to.'

'Don't take Ruddick for a fool, Timothy, she is sharp.'

'She is a servant wench. She will be glad of a comfortable bed and days with no work to do. The likes of her cannot better me.' He shook his head, Chloe thought it was as if he viewed Tobias as the fool.

Chloe was furious. She was about to speak up in defence of her man and retaliate, but Tobias stopped her.

'Live as you wish to, Timothy, until the day your lifestyle catches up with you. Then remember my words to you but it will be too late, or change now whilst you still can. I have chosen a different and happier path.'

'You'll rue the day, you mark my words. You need to stay ahead of the game, like me.' Timothy announced before riding off.

Chloe looked at Tobias who was not smiling. 'I am not ashamed of what we did, Tobias. You were right in everything you said. But are you sure you want to marry me?'

He leaned down and gently kissed her lips. 'Yes, I am, but not here, not now. In the summer, in my home village, with you dressed in the finest clothes, next to my mother. Our estate is small, it provides a comfortable income and our hearts are big.'

She smiled at him, and said sweetly,

'Then, my love, you may kiss me discreetly, but for all else we wait until the summer.' She kicked her horse onwards.

He rode alongside her. 'Only if you can resist my handsome face, my love.' He galloped ahead and she followed, laughing, knowing she would have to be strong for both of them without really caring if she was, so long as they were together and free.

★   ★   ★

Timothy returned to the hall, he would miss that income but would still manage to fund his new amusement. There would be no need to play the tables so much anyway now that he had a new interest. His man took his coat, gloves, hat and brought him a port on a silver salver with a letter laid upon it.

He sat in his favourite chair and downed the drink in one satisfied gulp, then turned his attention to his name, written he guessed by a feminine hand.

Opening the paper out, he relaxed into the chair, feeling the warmth from the fire.

He read the words once . . . then twice. The little minx, he thought and walked straight out of the hall to Ruddick's room, He slammed the door open. It hit the wall behind, rebounding it nearly hit his face, but fortunately his reactions were still as sharp as they had been when he served in Portugal. She'd gone. 'Damnation!' he swore, then made for the stable, 'Jimmy, re-saddle my . . . ' As he strode over to the cobbled square he saw his horse still by the water trough where he had left it not half an hour earlier — still saddled. 'Jimmy!' he shouted as he stormed through the stables, 'I'll take my crop to you, you lazy . . . '

He saw the futility of his threats as he reached the end stall. No Jimmy, no hat or coat on his peg. He too had flown the nest. Now he knew how Amelia aimed to reach York.

He shook his head and stared at the

sky as he leaned against the stable door watching Tobias return with the Branton wench. She dismounted into his arms, briefly, before returning to her room in the kitchens, no doubt, he thought to gloat to Cook.

Tobias walked both horses into the stables.

'Timothy, are you all right?' he asked, as he led each animal to his own stall.

'No!' he held up the letter to his friend. 'If you say you told me so, I swear I shall raise my crop to you.'

Tobias shrugged. 'Wouldn't dream of it — knowing it is enough.'

'I deserved that, I suppose.' Timothy walked over to the horse trough.

'What are you going to do?'

'Let her think she has the upper hand.' He let the letter drop into the water, the ink drifting away. He looked up at Tobias, 'I shall free her father, his debt is not great, then wrap myself up in her gratitude.'

'You think you can melt her heart so easily?' Tobias asked.

'I know it,' he said confidently, 'but she doesn't — yet.' He smiled.

'Give up gambling, Timothy.'

'I shall let Miss Ruddick mend my ways, as the Branton wench has done yours.' He nodded to the kitchens where Chloe had re-emerged clutching her precious bag.

'I don't think so, Timothy,' Tobias said, 'because I shall marry her, not use her. I want to settle down, with Chloe.'

Timothy remounted his horse. 'I must ride to free a man and hear what my fate will be in the woman's hands.' He beamed. 'I shall let her abuse my good nature, then, when the time is right, I shall claim my prize, within the month — I'll wager.'

'You think so?' Tobias stroked the horse's side.

'Bet you ten guineas I do . . . '

'You are giving up gambling, remember,' Tobias watched him as he winked back at him, waved to Chloe, then rode back out of the estate.

Chloe walked over to Tobias and saw

the paper floating in the trough. 'What is that?' she asked.

'The passage to a new adventure for Timothy and possibly his salvation or his ruin.'

Chloe placed her hand in his, 'You worry about your friend.'

He looked down at her and gently stroked her cheek. 'I have lost too many in the war, Chloe.' He looked up at the sky, knowing time had moved on. 'I shall get my things and then we shall be on our way. It is time my friend learned to live his own life, and we returned to ours.'

She watched him go into the stable and stared up at the sky, remembering those precious moments on the beach together, anticipating that with Tobias, her friend and fiancé, there would be many more to come.

We do hope that you have enjoyed
reading this large print book.

Did you know that all of our titles
are available for purchase?

We publish a wide range of high
quality large print books including:
Romances, Mysteries, Classics
General Fiction
Non Fiction and Westerns

Special interest titles available in
large print are:
The Little Oxford Dictionary
Music Book, Song Book
Hymn Book, Service Book

Also available from us courtesy of
Oxford University Press:
Young Readers' Dictionary
(large print edition)
Young Readers' Thesaurus
(large print edition)

For further information or a free
brochure, please contact us at:
Ulverscroft Large Print Books Ltd.,
The Green, Bradgate Road, Anstey,
Leicester, LE7 7FU, England.
Tel: (00 44) **0116 236 4325**
Fax: (00 44) **0116 234 0205**

HER HEART'S DESIRE

Chrissie Loveday

Zara and her friend, Lynne, have a catering business, which is growing in reputation. The enigmatic Oliver Pendlebury offers her a contract, but there are strings attached. Should she trust him? The demanding, pushy Amanda claims to be his fiancée — so can Zara really believe his denial? Besides, she has no time for romance. Oliver's world is so different to her own, and her biggest ambition is for the business to be a success. Which desire will win?

MISTAKE

Fene

When Emma ... o
unknown gent ... m
orchard she g ... m
was Lord Der ... ıis
companion o ... rd
Denver improved on acquaintance
and Emma believed that he returned
her affections — until he treated her
cruelly. She left the vicarage broken-
hearted. Would Richard find a way
to change her mind?